OUR SIXTH-GRADE SUGAR BABIES

Eve Bunting

HarperTrophy
A Division of HarperCollins*Publishers*

Our Sixth-Grade Sugar Babies
Copyright © 1990 by Eve Bunting
For information address HarperCollins Children's Books, a division of
HarperCollins Publishers, 10 East 53rd Street, New York, NY 10022.

Library of Congress Cataloging-in-Publication Data
Bunting, Eve, date
    Our sixth-grade sugar babies / Eve Bunting.
       p.   cm.
    Summary: Vicki and her best friend fear that their sixth-grade
project, carrying around five-pound bags of sugar to learn about
parental responsibility, will make them look ridiculous in the eyes
of the seventh-grade boy they both love.
    ISBN 0-397-32451-0.—ISBN 0-397-32452-9 (lib. bdg.)
    [1. Schools—Fiction.]   I. Title.
PZ7.H922Ou   1990   90-5487
[Fic]—dc20   CIP
                                                                    AC

A Scott Foresman Edition
ISBN 0-673-80138-1

Printed in the U.K.

To our own sugar babies:
Tory Bunting and Erin Bunting

OUR SIXTH-GRADE SUGAR BABIES

1

My friend Ellie and I were walking to school when HE came cycling down his driveway.

"Oh migosh," Ellie whispered. "Hide the sugar."

There was no way to hide the sugar. She and I were each carrying a five-pound sack of the stuff in see-through plastic bags. And you can't exactly shove a five-pound bag of anything under your sweater and still look normal.

"Hi," HE said.

"Er, hi," I said.

"Hi," Ellie echoed in a small voice beside me.

And then HE was gone, fast as that, cycling hard up Prescott Street, leaving us with a view of the back of a bright-red shirt and his blue-jeaned legs pumping the pedals.

Mr. Ambrose, who was standing on the sidewalk as usual, waved as HE went by. Mr. Ambrose smiles and waves at everyone who passes, on foot, on bike, or in a car. Mr. Ambrose waves at planes and helicopters.

HE waved back.

"Oh migosh, Vicki." Ellie sounded as if she might be about to faint. "HE spoke to us."

I nodded, overcome myself. I'd been just about to tell Ellie the great idea that had come to me last night like a thunderbolt from heaven. The one that was going to help me win the big argument with Mom. But the sight of HIM had put even the great idea out of my head.

HE had just moved into the house across the street from me two days ago. Ellie and I had spotted him immediately when he came out to talk to the moving-van man. He had dark curly hair, and even though we weren't that close, Ellie swore she'd seen a dimple in his chin. We'd had a hard time deciding what color his eyes were since we were so far away. I thought brown. Ellie thought dark blue. We were both hoping Ellie was right. After a lot of deliberation we'd agreed that he was probably a year or two older than we are, maybe thirteen. Maybe in junior high. We also agreed that he looked way more mature than the boys we're used to in Tilman Elementary.

"Blue or brown?" I asked Ellie now, as soon as we'd recovered our walking legs and our voices.

"It was too fast for me," Ellie said. "But there is definitely a dimple in his chin."

"And he has real dark eyebrows. I noticed that. And . . ." I stopped, horrified. "Ellie? How were my ears? Were they OK?" I began feeling in their general direction, pulling my hair forward to hide them. My Dumbo ears are my two biggest problems in life, requiring constant vigilance.

"I think they were covered, Vicki. Honest I do. Besides, if we hadn't time to see his eyes, he wouldn't have had time to see your ears. Or my freckles."

We smiled reassuringly at each other. "Whew!"

"Whew!"

"We *did* have to be carrying these dorky bags of sugar," I said. "What do you think he thought? He couldn't miss seeing them."

I thumped the side of my fat, pink-and-white sugar bag. "It serves us right. We should have put these stupid things in our backpacks. Why are we carrying them anyway?"

"Because Mrs. Oda said to carry them," Ellie said. "You don't put babies in backpacks. Besides, we didn't know we were going to meet somebody important."

"Mrs. Oda and her dumb projects," I said, forgetting that last night I'd decided this project was pretty terrific and could solve everything for me.

"Yeah! How does Mrs. Oda *think* of this dumb stuff?" Ellie asked.

Usually we don't talk this way about Mrs. Oda, our sixth-grade teacher. We think Mrs. Oda's OK. In fact, we've decided we want to look exactly like her when we get older, which doesn't seem too probable since neither of us is off to such a great start.

Mr. Ambrose saw us coming now and began waving. "Lovely day," he called. "Doesn't look like rain." Mr. Ambrose always says that, or something about the weather. Since this is Southern California, his greeting doesn't change much.

"Hi, Mr. Ambrose," we said.

His daughter, Ophelia, was out watering her roses. She twisted the hose nozzle so we wouldn't get sprayed as we passed.

"Hi, Vicki. Hi, Ellie. What's with the sugar? Are you baking cookies in homemaking class?"

I shook my head. "We don't *have* homemaking class. This is a school project. We have to carry these bags everywhere with us for a week."

Ellie made a face. "And this is only Monday, the first day. It's so embarrassing."

Ophelia picked a bug off a rose leaf and squashed it between her fingers. "You have to take them *everywhere*?"

"Around school, after school," Ellie said.

"Why?" Ophelia asked.

"To teach us responsibility," I said. "If we go to the mall, our sugar babies go too."

"If we go to the movies or shopping with our moms . . ." Ellie added.

Ophelia grinned. "That's what you call them? Your sugar babies?"

Ellie spread out her hands, which isn't easy when you're carrying a five-pound bag of sugar.

"*We* don't call them that," she said. "Mrs. Oda does. And she says we can only ask our moms to keep them once this whole week. She said our moms and dads are the babies' grandparents, and parents should never impose on grandparents."

A car came cruising by, and Mr. Ambrose waved happily. The driver slowed, staring out, probably wondering if he knew Mr. Ambrose and deciding there was a chance he did so he'd better wave back, just in case. Mr. Ambrose smiled and waved some more.

I can remember when Mr. Ambrose was an important businessman and went off to work every morning in a gray suit. Then things changed and he got a little bit strange. Once he wandered away and was lost for a whole day. The police had to bring him back.

Ophelia is a nurse, and she was working in Oakland then. But she gave up her job right away and came back here to live with her father.

I used to feel sorry for Mr. Ambrose, but now I've decided that he's as happy as can be, standing out in the sun, keeping busy waving and smiling. He's a plus for the neighborhood, because he makes everybody who passes happier, too.

"What happens if you get asked on a date?" Ophelia asked, cocking her head and looking like a big, perky jay in her bright-blue sweatshirt. "Does Sugar Baby go along?"

"Oh, we don't have to worry about that. We never get asked on dates," Ellie said quickly.

"You don't have to tell the world, Ellie," I said. "It could happen. Maybe."

"Speaking of which," Ophelia added, "have you met that nice-looking new boy who's moved into the Sobel house?"

"Oh . . . ah . . . sort of," I said, shooting a quick glance in Ellie's direction. "Have you met him, Ophelia?"

Ophelia fussed with the nozzle of the hose, adjusting it to a fine spray that made a fizzle of rainbows in the air. "I've met his parents," she said. "Their name is Shub. The father's a professor in Santa Cruz, but he's here for a year on an exchange to Caltech. I think they have two boys."

"*Two* boys?" Ellie squeaked. Her face turned pink with excitement. Ellie says the kind of skin that has lots of freckles is also prone to lots of pinking up.

"Sorry," Ophelia said. "One of the boys is real little."

I smoothed my hair over my ears, checking that they weren't sticking up like shark fins in water. "You didn't happen to find out the older boy's name, did you?" I asked casually.

Ophelia grinned. "No. Now how could I have forgotten to ask something that important? He's in junior high, though, his mother did say that. Seventh grade. In fact, I think I just saw him ride by on his way to school this morning."

"Seventh grade? Really?" I said in a disinterested voice. "Well, I guess we'd better go, Ellie. Bye, Ophelia."

"Yeah. We don't want to be late."

We waved good-bye to Mr. Ambrose.

"Just like we thought," said Ellie. "HE's in seventh grade. And you know who else is in the seventh grade? Lisa Bartone, from last year. And that cute Cynthia Sanders." Ellie looked glum. "They'll spot him fast and he'll spot them. Lisa and Cynthia are boy magnets."

"Still," I said, "I'm going to be living opposite him for a whole year. And you're on the same street."

"The same *side* even." Ellie shifted her bag of sugar. "Can you believe this thing weighs only five pounds? It feels like five tons."

"Does yours feel heavier now than when we started?" I asked.

"Ten times heavier."

I turned, walking sideways so I could see Ellie's face as I talked. "Listen, I was going to tell you before, but HE put it right out of my head. About the sugar babies. You know how my mom and I have been arguing?"

"Because she won't let you go to look after Keiko in the summer?"

I nodded. Keiko is my little half sister. My dad married Keiko's mom and lives with them in Waterloo, Iowa.

"Well, you know I've been trying and trying to get Mom to change her mind, and she won't. She says I'm not old enough, and it's too much responsibility." I paused for breath. "But now, if I can look after this sugar baby for a whole week—if I do it really well and even get an A in responsibility, then how can she—"

10

Ellie interrupted me. She and I interrupt each other all the time. It's kind of our style. "But Vicki, will you even want to go to Iowa now that HE's here? I mean, he'll be hanging around, riding his bike, doing stuff—maybe even doing stuff with *us*."

We cradled our sugar babies extra tight and rolled our eyes, imagining.

"Well . . ." I thought about how terrific it would be to be fully in charge of little Keiko in the daytime, making decisions, being almost like an adult. I could boss her around, and there'd be nobody there to boss *me* around. We'd eat what we wanted. I'd read her stories and we'd go out and we'd be real, true sisters. Last year I'd stayed with them for five days. Of course, Dad and Yoshi, Keiko's mother, were there all the time, too. But this year I'd have Keiko to myself, every single day, and they'd only be there nights. As if that wasn't wonderful enough, Dad was going to pay me for baby-sitting. A hundred dollars for two weeks! When Dad first asked me, and before Mom said "No," I'd lain awake for hours, planning how to spend it.

"Yes, Ellie, I'd still want to go. HE will be here the whole summer. I'd be gone for only two weeks."

"You mean 'Thunk' will be here," Ellie said.

"Huh?"

" 'Thunk.' Isn't that a great name? I made it up.

T for Terrific. HUNK. We can use it till we find out his real one."

I beamed. "Ellie! I love it. Thunk Shub." The two sounds together were like someone taking the lid off a jar of Vaseline and putting it on again. Thunk Shub. It was perfect.

2

The questions started as soon as we got close to school. Kids who knew us—and kids who didn't—were all calling out:

"How come you've got bags of sugar?"

"Are you doing an art project?"

"Is it for a food drive? Sugar's not that good for you, you know. It rots your teeth."

Ellie and I tried to ignore them and stay cool and superior, especially if they were little third or fourth graders. I mean, *really!*

There was a bag of sugar on every desk in Mrs. Oda's room.

"Look what Judy did with hers!" Tina Fisher said as soon as we came in. Judy held up her sugar baby for us to admire. She'd sewn it into a white cloth bag, on which she had painted a face with red lips, bugged-out blue eyes, and black curls. Judy had drawn in a shirt, with a collar and buttons down the front, and a skirt with crayon lines for pleats.

13

She'd also drawn in legs, and there were red-strapped shoes where the feet should be.

"Her name's Corky," Judy said proudly.

"More like Porky," Jeremiah Green said.

Judy giggled. "She *is* kind of heavy."

"Fat legs," I said. "Cute, though." I glanced around. "Where's *your* sugar baby, Harry Hogan?"

Harry Hogan sits directly behind me, and he is the pain of my life. Harry Hogan has sat directly behind me in every class since the first grade, and he has been a pain all the way.

"Where's your sugar baby, Harry Hogan?" he repeated in this horrible, whiny voice he uses to echo everything I say.

"We're supposed to bring our babies today," I said coldly.

"We're supposed to bring our babies today," Harry whined, squeezing his mouth into the little rosebud shape that's not a bit like mine.

I turned my back on him and said, "Some people!"

"Some people!" Harry repeated with this affected snort of a laugh.

I think I hate Harry Hogan more than anybody in the whole world. It's so frustrating. There's no point in answering him back because he just repeats my answer and it goes on and on. Once I'd pretended not to hear and he'd said, "Don't say you can't hear," and I was afraid he might have been referring to my ears. But surely even Horrible Harry Hogan wouldn't be that horrible.

Mrs. Oda came through the door just then, calling out, "Good morning, class."

"Good morning, Mrs. Oda," we chirped back.

Mrs. Oda wears straight skirts and silk shirts to school every day. Ellie and I think it's very thoughtful when a teacher tries to dress nicely. After all, we have to look at her. This morning Mrs. Oda was wearing peach-colored lipstick that exactly matched her peachy blouse. She set her big denim carryall on her desk and rubbed her arm as if the bag had been heavy. Then she surveyed the room. Mrs. Oda never takes attendance. She says she can spot an empty desk in the flick of a lamb's tail, which I expect is very quick.

"Well," she said, "I see that most of you brought your sugar babies and most of you have wrapped them nicely in plastic as I suggested. We're hoping to be able to give the sugar back to your parents next week, clean and usable." Then she looked at Horrible Harry Hogan. "I don't see *your* sugar baby, Harry."

"I forgot, Mrs. Oda."

"Didn't you take home the paper I gave you? Didn't you show it to your parents?"

15

Harry took the pink paper that explained about the project from his desk.

"I forgot, Mrs. Oda."

Mrs. Oda made a face. "A very good thing we're starting a lesson on responsibility." She pulled a bag of sugar wrapped in plastic from her carryall. "Come up here, Harry. You may borrow this. But keep it clean. I want it back next Monday."

"Thanks." Harry swaggered up to her desk and swaggered back with the sugar.

"Poor kid, getting *him* for a father," Ellie whispered to me.

I raised my eyebrows. "Really!"

Judy Petrone held up Corky and said, "Look what I did, Mrs. Oda."

Mrs. Oda clapped her hands.

"That's perfect, Judy. You're really getting into the right spirit. There's just one problem, though. How do you know you have a girl? You don't get to choose, Judy. That's not the way it works in life."

"What do you mean?"

Mrs. Oda took a wide-topped jar from her bag. Inside it I could see bits of folded paper.

"Come up one at a time," she said. "Whether you get a boy or a girl depends on the luck of the draw. This row first. Victoria? We'll start with you."

16

She unscrewed the lid of the jar and I put my hand in and pulled out one of the paper slips. "Yeah!" I said, beaming around. "It's a girl."

"It's a girl!" Harry Hogan fluttered his eyelashes.

"Stop doing that, Harry, and come up and pull a slip for yourself," Mrs. Oda said.

Harry tried to fumble a slip open inside the jar and peek, but Mrs. Oda put her hand over his eyes. "Just take one, Harry."

"If I get a girl, I'll croak." Harry opened the paper and sighed with relief. "It's a boy. I got the good kind."

"Sit down, Harry," Mrs. Oda said.

George Cuesta got a boy, too. "Yeah!" he said. "My son's going to be a soccer player." George is a full-on soccer freak, and he's always captain of one of the playground teams at recess or lunch. He grinned, hooked a finger around the rubber band that stretches across his top teeth, and pinged.

George can play "God Bless America" and "Silent Night" on his rubber band. We do have the most disgusting boys in sixth grade. Not much wonder Ellie and I are attracted to more mature types— like Thunk.

When it was her turn to pick, Ellie showed me her fingers, crossed for luck. I crossed mine, too. But the charm didn't work.

"A boy!" Ellie said in disgust. "Are you sure you *have* any girl babies in there, Mrs. Oda?"

"I'm sure."

"*I* got a girl. Want to trade?" Paul Almaguer asked.

Ellie beamed, leaning across to exchange slips. Mrs. Oda shook her head. "Uh-uh. With real babies you don't just say, 'I don't like what I got,' and go next door to your neighbor's house and say, 'Let's trade.' No way. You keep what you were given."

"But I don't *want* a boy," Ellie wailed.

Lots of kids got the kind they didn't want. Poor Corky turned out to be a boy, too.

Jeremiah Green gave a horse laugh and pointed at Corky's pleated skirt and blouse and her little red shoes. "Love his outfit," he said.

"I'm going to have to make him a whole new set of clothes," Judy said sadly. "And he won't be half as cute."

"Unless you turn him into a Scottish boy wearing a kilt," Mrs. Oda suggested.

Judy shook her head. "How could he be Scottish? My whole family's Italian."

But the worst shock of all was still to come. Tina Fisher got twins.

"What is *this*? Twin girls? I have only one bag of sugar."

Mrs. Oda whipped another bag from her carryall and put it in Tina's arms. "Now you have two."

Tina looked shocked. "But how could this happen?"

Mrs. Oda laughed. "I imagine that's what every mother says when she discovers she has twins."

"You mean I have to lug *two* sugar sacks around with me everywhere for a whole *week*? That's not fair."

"Double your pleasure, double your fun, Tina, my dear," Mrs. Oda said.

Tina kept shaking her head and saying, "Oh, no. Oh, no." It was kind of funny. But I was glad I only had one.

Everyone was calling out what kind of baby they had to everyone else. Some were naming them already. It was Jeremiah Green who put up his hand first when Mrs. Oda asked if anybody had a question.

"You said we have to take our babies everywhere. I've got a girl. What do I do when I have to go to the bathroom? You should give boys to boys and girls to girls. That would be easier."

Mrs. Oda perched on the edge of her desk swinging her long, elegant legs. She always wears the prettiest shoes, narrow and cut low over her toes. She buys them in Robinson's. Ellie and I met her once in the mall carrying a Robinson's shoe box.

"Turn her face to the wall, Jeremiah, if you're that modest," she said. "Just no leaving her alone outside the bathroom door."

I looked down at my sugar baby. It was amazing the difference it made knowing she was a girl. Now she was a person. I took her off my desk and put her beside me. "I'm going to fix you up so nicely," I whispered. "You wait and see."

I wondered if my mom and dad had been pleased when they found out I was a girl. Was I what they'd wanted? Did they love each other then? They must have, surely. And when Dad and Yoshi had little Keiko, were they happy that it was another girl? Keiko is so sweet with her big, dark eyes and shy smile. When I came back last summer, I told Mom how sweet Keiko is, and how pretty. Mom had said, in a cool way, "Well, I imagine she looks like her mother. And I imagine Yoshi's very pretty too." It was sort of a question, but I didn't answer. Wouldn't it be hurtful to Mom to know how beautiful Yoshi is? I mean, if your husband leaves you and ends up marrying someone else, what you probably don't want to know is how beautiful that person is.

Mrs. Oda's voice cut through my thoughts.

"Are there any other questions?"

"Do we get graded on this?"

"Absolutely. This is a citizenship grade, and it's very important."

It was going to be very important to me, all right. It could make all the difference.

"How are you going to know if we cheat?" That was Horrible Harry Hogan, of course. "I mean, we could *say* we never left our sugar babies alone. How would you know? You wouldn't."

"I'm putting you on your honor. That's how I'll know. Trusting is the beginning of responsibility, and I trust every single one of you." I thought she smiled specially at me.

Ellie says she thinks I'm Mrs. Oda's pet, and I say, "Oh, no, *you're* her pet." Judy Petrone says she thinks Jeremiah Green is Mrs. Oda's favorite, but Ellie and I don't think that could be possible. My mom says an exceptional teacher makes every student in the class feel valued, and that's probably the way it is. Still, I privately feel Mrs. Oda likes me a lot.

Harry Hogan leaned forward and blew on the back of my head.

"Are you going to cheat, Victoria?"

"Of course not," I said. "I would never disappoint Mrs. Oda. I won't cheat, but *you* will. I'm positively certain about that, Harry Hogan."

Which just goes to show—you should never be positively certain about anything.

3

On Mondays and Wednesdays Ellie goes straight from school to the Y for swimming. We stood together on the steps of Tilman in the warm March sun, cradling our sugar babies.

"What am I going to do with Sweet Sam while I'm swimming?" Ellie asked me. "I can't leave him in my locker." Ellie had decided on Sweet Sam for her baby's name. I'd decided on Babe, which I thought was very cute and sporty sounding. I'd also decided that Babe had red hair and emerald-green eyes and the prettiest, littlest ears imaginable.

"If I bring him down by the pool, he'll get splashed. He might melt," Ellie said.

"Melt?" I was shocked. "I don't think he *would*, through plastic."

"Well, what if somebody tosses him in? There are some not very nice girls there from Poly who think it's smart to tease." Ellie's face had pinked up, so I knew she was upset. She kept patting Sweet Sam's shoulder.

"I'll keep him for you," I said. "That would be OK, wouldn't it? Sometimes a friend would keep your real baby if you had to go to the doctor or shopping or something. That makes sense."

Ellie beamed at me. "Let's keep each other's babies a couple of times this week."

"And when we grow up and have real babies, we'll do it, too," I said. "Because we'll always be best friends."

"And we'll live next door to each other," Ellie added. We knew that would be a condition of marrying our husbands. That, and being able to have our own Robinson's charge cards. "I'll be Aunt Ellie and you'll be Aunt Victoria."

We smiled happily at each other, imagining.

I held out my free arm. "This will be good practice. Come to Aunt Vicki, Sweet Sam."

"Be good," Ellie told him. "I'll pick him up on my way home," she told me.

"OK. See you later." I began walking. Man, were these babies heavy. The two of them were weighing me down in front, and my backpack was weighing me down behind. I'd never thought it was so far from school to my street. Twice I had to stop and put Babe and Sweet Sam down so I could ease my arms. Poor Tina, I thought. Awful to have twins. One baby was bad enough. I kept myself going thinking about how I'd be passing Thunk's house on the way home. I wouldn't see him, of course, because the junior high kids get out later than we do. But even his house seemed magic now. I was thinking that I could conveniently be in my yard later, about four, when Thunk might come whizzing by, and I could maybe shout "Hi" again, or even something else. Except right now I couldn't think of anything else to shout.

Mr. Ambrose was out on the sidewalk as usual, and as usual he waved to me as soon as I rounded the corner. I always wave back, but today I had no free arms.

As soon as I got close enough, I called "Hello."

"Beautiful today," he said. "Lots of sunshine."

"Lots of sunshine." My echo reminded me of Horrible Harry Hogan, only I wasn't being nasty and Horrible Harry Hogan was, all the time.

One good thing about Mr. Ambrose, he is not passremarkable. I mean, he doesn't pass remarks. There I was with two big bags of sugar and he didn't say a thing, just turned his wonderful gentle smile on me.

Down the street a ways I saw the little Garcia boy peering out from his oleander hedge. He had on his cowboy boots and hat and I distinctly saw his water pistol in his hand, though I know for a fact his mom has told him that his water pistol is never to go beyond their front yard. I think she and Mr. Garcia have had complaints. I was glad I didn't have to go that far, as I've been ambushed with that water pistol more than once.

"Mr. Ambrose," I said, "this is my baby, Babe. And this is Sweet Sam. Say hello to Mr. Ambrose, children."

"Hello," I said in a baby voice, raising the arm that held Babe.

I raised Sweet Sam. "Hello, Mr. Ambrose."

"Yes, sir, lovely day." Mr. Ambrose gazed blissfully at the haze of mountains that floated against the sky.

"I've thought of a way to convince Mom," I told him. "Remember? I was telling you how she doesn't want to let me go to Waterloo to look after Keiko, remember? Dad and Yoshi are going to be artists for two weeks at that fancy summer school, and Dad wants me to stay with my little sister. We got along so well together last summer. Mom doesn't want me to go because she says it's too much responsibility for me, though I have a strong suspicion that's not the only reason."

Mr. Ambrose smiled dreamily, face lifted to the sun.

"But—if I can look after Babe perfectly, every minute, for one whole week, Mom will have to give in. Right?"

A gardening truck came rattling by, and Mr. Ambrose wakened to wave to it.

"Where was I?" I asked.

Ophelia says Mr. Ambrose likes to be talked to, and I sure like talking to him. She says she's not certain how much her father understands, but that she makes a point of presuming he understands everything, and maybe he does. She says the doctor says that's the best thing we can do for him, and I for one like doing it. Once I even had a long conversation with Mr. Ambrose about my father and how I miss him. "Not him so much," I'd explained, "because I don't really remember him. He and my mom got divorced when I was two. It's the *idea* of a father that I miss. Like, when I see other kids with *their* dads. I even feel a bit jealous of Keiko, because she has her mom and dad, too. But what the heck, Mr. Ambrose. Mom and I do OK. And we're all happy now, I guess. Besides, lots of kids have only one parent."

Mr. Ambrose had smiled and nodded, and when

I'd finished, he'd said in the sweetest way, "Feels like spring, doesn't it?"

Afterward I'd realized that I tell Mr. Ambrose things I don't tell anyone else. Not even Mom, or Ellie.

Ellie says Mr. Ambrose is easy to talk to because he never gives silly advice or says if you're right or wrong. He never makes you feel dumb. Ellie's probably right.

I gazed across the street, at Thunk's house. "Isn't it funny, Mr. Ambrose? I never really looked at that house before. It's pretty, isn't it? I like the way the vines creep around the top of the porch. And I bet that's a nice little room up there, like an attic under the roof. Do you think maybe it's Thunk's room?"

Mr. Ambrose waved at the Mitchells' beagle that had escaped from their yard as usual and was happily chasing shadows on the opposite sidewalk.

I lowered my voice. "I might come out later on, too, and talk with you some more, Mr. Ambrose. Accidentally-on-purpose, at the exact time junior high lets out, OK? I was going to spy from my yard, but right here is even better. Closer. Perfectly opposite Thunk's."

"Lovely day," Mr. Ambrose said enthusiastically.

"Yes, sir."

"I'll have to bring Babe and Sweet Sam. Did I tell you, by the way, that Babe has bright-green eyes and fabulous red hair? And although I'm her mother, she's going to miss out on my baboon ears. Sometimes big-ear genes skip a generation, and Babe is in the skip year. I just wish *I'd* been in the skip year."

Mr. Ambrose watched a cloud that sailed high and white over the treetops. "We call the new boy Thunk because he's a terrific hunk," I said. "Isn't that clever? Ellie thought of it. Thunk Shub."

Something rustled in Ophelia's camellia bush behind me, and my heart gave a little jump. Then a kid in a cowboy hat came around the side of the shrubbery. He had one of those red cowboy scarves tied across the bottom of his face, too, like a mask. All I could see were blue eyes behind round, pale-rimmed glasses. I glanced down the street. The Garcia boy was still there, peering from his hedge. This had to be one of his friends, and they'd been playing bandit or something. My heart gave another, nastier jump. He must have heard me babbling on to Mr. Ambrose. What had I said? What?

I smiled winningly. "Oh, hi. I didn't see you. You scared me for a minute."

He pulled down the red bandanna and pushed back his hat. I'd never seen him before, and I thought

I knew all the little kids around here. This one must be from the next block, or . . . Something even more horrifying was edging itself into my mind. No! Please, no! Couldn't be! "Oh, ah . . . by any chance have you just moved in across the . . . over there?" I asked, nodding in the general direction of Thunk's house, shaking my head to encourage him to shake his and tell me that no, I was totally wrong.

"Yeah," he said. "We just moved in."

My arms were aching with all this standing in one place holding these two heavy weights, and I jiggled them a little so that the sugar babies bounced and settled.

The little kid's eyes darted from my face to them, then back to me.

"Well, look," I said, "I don't want you to get the wrong idea. I didn't know you were there. . . . I mean, behind me in the bushes and . . ." My mind was going around and around like a carousel. I remembered I'd talked about the nice little room that might be Thunk's and how I'd come out here later, because here was closer and, oh heavens, that part about why Ellie and I had christened him Thunk.

I swallowed. "You see, in school we got these babies . . ." I began.

"I gotta go." He was walking backward, never once taking his eyes off me.

"Look," I said again, "it's not nice to sneak around and listen to other—"

"I wasn't sneaking. I'm Jesse James, and I'm hiding from the posse."

He turned, racing down the sidewalk in the direction of his new friend, stopping once to look back at me and make a loopy sign with his finger against the side of his head.

"Do you think he heard *everything*, Mr. Ambrose?" I moaned aloud. "About Thunk and even about my ears? I might as well have stuck a flag in each one if I'd wanted to draw attention to them. Can you imagine him telling his brother? 'There's this girl. She must live close. She carries around two bags of sugar and she talks to them. And she and her friend think you're a Thunk, Thunk.' What am I going to do, Mr. Ambrose? I'm so humiliated."

Mr. Ambrose was looking at me with such pity that I was sure he understood. I waited for a weather remark that didn't come. For once even Mr. Ambrose was speechless.

4

All I wanted to do now was get home and hide. And maybe tell Mom the awful thing that had happened.

When I got to our house, I saw that there was a car that wasn't ours in the driveway, which meant that Mom had a client. Getting sympathy from her would have to wait. Mom's a CPA, a certified public accountant. She likes what she does, preparing people's taxes, but she says her job is like a dentist's. Everyone puts off coming to her till the last minute, so the last minutes are the pits. Since this is March, the pits are here. Mom works from our house, and when her office door is closed, I stay away. "Unless it's an emergency or extreme disaster, Victoria," I've been told a million times. This was both, but I wasn't sure it would qualify with her.

The kitchen clock said ten after four now. Thunk time. But no way was I going outside to watch for him. After what had happened, I might never go outside again.

I fixed myself some raisin toast and moped around, going over and over what I'd said. And the more I thought about it, the worse it got. I felt myself pinking up with embarrassment. Unfortunately, people who don't have freckles can pink up too.

After a while I made myself pay attention to poor Babe and Sweet Sam, who'd been dumped on the kitchen table. I set them side by side in a chair, then rummaged in Mom's ragbag for something suitable for Babe to wear. There was an old T-shirt that I'd had back in second grade when I went to day camp at Singing Pines. Once it had been white, but it had suffered the same fate as most of our laundry and had gone through the cycle with something red. Now it was a pretty pale pink. I'd just finished sewing Babe into it and telling her how much better she'd look if she had a head when Ellie knocked on the kitchen window.

I rushed to let her in.

"Thank goodness you're here," I gasped, dragging her by the arm. "The most awful thing you can think of happened to me on the way—"

"Did you see HIM?" Ellie asked.

"You mean Thunk? That's what I'm trying to tell you. I—"

"You didn't see him out there? Now? With her?"

"Thunk? He's out there now? With somebody?"

Ellie looked grim. "Didn't I tell you? Didn't I say this would happen?"

"Who? What?" I was already heading for our living room, which has a nice secret view of the street from behind its miniblinds. Then I remembered the babies. "Wait. We have to bring them," I said.

Through the narrow slats of the blinds we watched Thunk, standing at the end of his driveway, his bicycle propped against a palm tree while he smiled in a very animated way at that vulture, Cynthia Sanders.

"You *said* she'd spot him straight off," I said mournfully. "You said she was a boy magnet. She must have walked him home. Can you believe it?"

We pulled our eyes from Thunk to stare in amazement at each other. "How do you suppose she asked him? 'Can I walk you to your house, Thunk?' I didn't think even Cynthia Sanders would have that much nerve."

"Maybe she told him she lived on this street."

"But she doesn't."

"Yes, but maybe she said she did. Some girls will say anything."

"Really! I guess we're lucky Lisa Bartone didn't walk him home, too."

Babe was getting heavy, so I set her down on the blue-velvet couch. Ellie put Sweet Sam beside her.

"I see you've started fixing Babe up," Ellie said. I nodded, but right now our hearts and our interests were not on our sugar babies. We went back to our posts at the window.

Across the street Thunk was smiling a delicious white-toothed smile at Cynthia Sanders. It was enough to chill my blood. Cynthia was wearing black tights with Converse high tops and a big yellow shirt with a dangling silver belt.

"I think her legs are too skinny for those tights," I said. "I can see a droop, even."

"I don't think that's a droop, I think it's a muscle. Cynthia Sanders has great leg muscles."

Cynthia had picked up a magnolia pod and was examining it carefully, showing something to Thunk.

Ellie groaned. "Look how *fake*! You'd think she'd never *seen* a magnolia pod in her life before."

"The whole street is littered with them," I said. "Honestly. What a rare archaeological find." Now

Thunk was examining the pod too, his head bent close to Cynthia's. "He looks as though *he's* never seen a magnolia pod before," I said.

"Maybe they don't have magnolias where he came from," Ellie suggested.

I nodded. "Probably not."

"Cynthia Sanders isn't really all that pretty," Ellie said.

"Her feet are awfully big." I craned my neck for a better view. "Of course, they could be normal size. It might be just those high tops."

We watched, mesmerized, as Cynthia lifted the dangling end of her silver conch belt to show Thunk.

"I mean, *really*," Ellie said. "It's not exactly an Aztec treasure. You can buy those belts for $2.95 in KMart. Cam has one." Cam is Ellie's thirteen-year-old sister. Ellie has three sisters and three brothers. She's right in the middle like the cheese in the sandwich.

"I could probably borrow Cam's if I wanted," she added thoughtfully.

Thunk wound the end of the belt around his finger, and I was ready to die of jealousy.

"We should get out in front ourselves and be noticed," Ellie said. "It's no good skulking in here, giving that Cynthia Sanders a head start."

"Out there? Are you kidding? You haven't even *heard* what happened! Wait—" I gave Ellie a quick, thumbnail summary of my humiliation.

Her eyes widened. "Are you certain sure he heard?"

"I'm positive."

She bit her lip and I bit mine, and we went back to skulking and watching.

"And you said *I* made up the name?" Ellie asked after a minute.

I nodded. "I'm sorry, El. I thought I was telling only Mr. Ambrose."

Ellie nibbled her lips some more.

"Did that Cynthia Sanders even speak to you when you went past?" I asked.

"Of course not." Ellie tweaked one of her wet spikes of hair. "Would you speak to me?"

I have to admit, Ellie is not at her best after swimming. The chlorine doesn't bleach her freckles. It bleaches everything else, so the freckles really stand out. Ellie says chlorine brings out freckles she doesn't even *have* and she may have to give up swimming altogether. Ellie says after swimming she reminds herself of a Dalmatian pup. Also, after swimming Ellie never takes time to put herself together right and has been known to put her clothes on back to front or outside in. Right now her blouse was buttoned into the wrong buttonholes so one end dropped down.

"We need a plan," Ellie said, twirling the wand of the miniblind so the slats opened and closed. "We'll go out and rake leaves on your lawn. And Cynthia will call out, 'Hi, Vicki. Hi, Ellie. Come on over here.'"

"Sure she will," I said. "And anyway, what leaves are we raking? There are no leaves."

"We'll rake the grass."

"How can you rake grass when it hasn't been cut?" I fixed the buttons on her blouse.

"We'll plant flowers. No, we'll dig up flowers. We'll weed. Do you know which are weeds? We'll— we'll take out the Frisbee and start throwing it on the street and we'll throw it over there so we can go get it and—"

"And we'll look like a couple of klutzes," I said. "Forget it. Anyway, I'm in hiding."

"You're wrong," Ellie said. "Now's the perfect time for you to get over there and meet him. Thunk's just coming home from school. His kid brother hasn't even seen him yet. This is your chance to show him you're perfectly normal. And nice. And cute."

"And live across the street," I added, getting carried away myself. She was right. We should stake our claim before Cynthia Sanders had him totally trapped.

"Let's think. Let's think." I rapped the side of my head with my fist. "We need something believable. And cool. And mature."

"Look!" Ellie pointed. The Mitchells' beagle was trotting along the opposite sidewalk and Thunk had crouched to pet him.

"I like boys who like dogs," Ellie said.

I giggled. "You mean, if he likes dogs, he should like us? Only kidding," I added quickly, because it really wasn't funny to joke about something that close to the truth.

"If you had a dog, we could walk him."

"But I don't. If only we had something important about school that Cynthia . . ." I stopped. "Ellie! I've just had the best idea."

"You're snorting, Victoria," Ellie warned. I snort when I get excited, and I've alerted Ellie to point it out when I do so I can stop. I took a deep breath. "Last year's play program," I said.

Ellie looked at me blankly.

"*Beauty and the Beast*, starring Cynthia Sanders," I explained. "You know how I'm in charge of the bulletin board publicity for this year's play? And remember how Judy Petrone said we should put last year's program up there along with last year's newspaper clippings?" I grabbed Ellie's arm. "Don't you think an autographed program would be even better? Autographed by one of the stars."

Ellie beamed at me. "Genius."

"I'll get the program right now," I said. "You can take it over and tell her we want it autographed for the display. We'll plan exactly what you should—"

"*Me* take it over? Oh, no. *You* take it over, Victoria."

Across the street Thunk was fondling the beagle's ears.

Ellie and I sighed and looked at each other. There was no need for words.

"You should be the one to go anyway," Ellie said. "It's your idea and your program and your house and your bulletin board and—"

"And my *pen*," I said sarcastically. "OK, we'll both go, then. But I'm warning you, if that little kid's anywhere in sight, I'm turning back. Truly."

"But if we both go, we'll have to take Sweet Sam and Babe," Ellie reminded me. "Then we'll look like a couple of dweebs."

"No kidding," I said.

"So I'll baby-sit them and you go. Get the program

fast, though, Vicki. They're not going to stand out there forever."

I stalled for time. "Maybe I should wait till Cynthia goes," I began.

"Oh, sure. What good would that do? You'd ask *Thunk* to sign her picture on last year's play program? Get real, Vicki. And you should go now. Is the program still stuck in your dresser mirror? I'll get it. You keep an eye on them."

I was hoping Cynthia Sanders would take off before I could go over there, but the only one to leave was the Mitchells' dog.

When Ellie came back, we studied the program. TILMAN ELEMENTARY PRESENTS: BEAUTY AND THE BEAST. No need to mention that Cynthia did not play the part of the beast. Underneath was the picture of Cynthia with Tom McCartney, who did, and who was really pretty cute, too, even in his Beast makeup. "It's a good shot of Cynthia," I said mournfully.

"Don't think about it." Ellie jammed the program and my Papermate pen into my hands, fixed my hair over my ears, and pulled my T-shirt out so it bagged in front. This is a trick she and I use to pretend there's more hidden under there than there really is. My heart was twit-twittering.

"But what will I say?"

"Say . . ." Ellie stepped back, examined me with her head on one side, then bagged my T-shirt some more.

"Say, 'I saw you over here, Cynthia, and I thought it would be a good chance—'"

"A good opportunity," I corrected. "It sounds more professional. Anyway, I can think of what to say to *her*. It's Thunk I'm worried about. What will I say to *him*?"

"Say, 'Welcome to Pasadena.'"

"No way. That's what *my* mom would say to *his* mom. Besides, he—"

"Well, say, 'Isn't it nice and warm today?'"

"That's probably what Mr. Ambrose told him already."

"I know. Say, 'That's my house across the street. My name's Victoria, and I've lived here for ages and ages. If you want to know where anything is around here, come on over and—'"

I rolled my eyes. "Oh, sure. I can just hear me. Ellie, I don't want to do this. I don't think I can."

"Yes, you can," Ellie said. "But take a deep breath and stop snorting."

I took a deep breath.

What had I gotten myself into?

5

Ellie was pushing me from behind the way a bulldozer pushes a pile of trash, and I was suddenly outside with the front door closed behind me. And there they were—the two of them, Cynthia and Thunk—laughing and talking.

I glanced to the right and breathed easier. Two small cowboys on scooters were careening along the sidewalk a block and a half away. To the left, Mr. Ambrose checked the sky for impending storms.

I clutched the pen and the program in my sweaty hands and crossed the street.

Thunk and Cynthia stopped talking as I got closer. I walked slower. What was I doing here? I wanted to turn and run, but it was too late.

"Hi, Cynthia," I muttered. And to Thunk, "Er, hi."

I couldn't believe it when they both said "Hi" back. Cynthia even smiled.

"Is that last year's play program?" she asked, sounding interested.

"Ah, yes." I held it so she could see it better. "Remember me? I'm Vicki Charlip. From Tilman."

Cynthia kind of hesitated and then said quickly, "From Tilman? Sure."

More than my hands were sweating now. Why had I asked if she remembered me? Of course she didn't remember me. What was there to remember? At least she hadn't said no, thank goodness.

"I'm trying to get autographs, you know, from last year's cast. I'm going to display the program beside this year's program on the bulletin board. I'm in charge of publicity and . . ." I was going to say Cynthia's picture would be a big attraction, but it probably wouldn't be very smart to point that out to Thunk. Instead I let the sentence slide away and glanced at him sideways. Oh, wow. He was even cuter up close! He had his hand out for the program, and I gave it to him, smiling up at him in a sickening sort of way. I can't stand girls who smile sickeningly at boys, but what the heck. I'm not sure he saw anyway. He was too busy admiring Cynthia's picture.

"I like your hair better the way you have it now," he told her.

I would *die* if a boy said something that nice to

44

me, but Cynthia just tossed off a "thanks" in the most casual way imaginable. I decided Ellie and I ought to practice that in case a compliment ever came our way.

"We did *Jack in the Beanstalk* in our school last year," Thunk said.

"Were you in it?" Cynthia asked.

Thunk grinned. "Yeah. I was the beanstalk."

I laughed very loudly and said, "I'm sure," also very loudly to show him what a good sense of humor I had, and also to show I knew he was kidding about being the beanstalk. He smiled down at me and I almost passed out. His eyes *were* blue. Ellie had been right about that and she'd been right about the dimple, too. Thunk was perfect.

Well, actually, he had some little bumps on his chin, right next to the dimple. We hadn't noticed those as he'd steamed past us this morning on his bicycle. They weren't pimples exactly, or at least not the gross kind. These were more like hives, or mosquito bites. I decided it was probably better that he wasn't flawless. It made him more possible.

"Do you have a pen?" Cynthia asked me.

"A pen?" I couldn't figure out what she was talking about. Then I remembered the reason I was supposed to be here. "Oh, yes, a pen." I gave it to her.

"Where do you want me to sign it?"

"Just across the front." Two or three more seconds and I'd have no reason to hang around anymore. Think fast, Vicki. "Ah, maybe you could put something else on there, Cynthia, like about having good memories of the play or about . . . about how you felt when everybody clapped or . . .' "

"Um." Cynthia chewed on the end of my pen and stared into space.

Now was my chance to grab onto Thunk while she was thinking.

I checked my ears with my fingertip, then risked a glance across at my house for courage. The blind slats gave a reassuring flick. Ellie and the sugar babies were with me in spirit.

"How do you think you'll like it here?" I asked Thunk.

"I don't know yet," Thunk said. "It seems OK."

I nodded understandingly.

"I'm feeling really dumb," Cynthia said. "I can't think of a thing to write."

"How about 'Wherever I wander, wherever I roam,' " Thunk suggested, "then put the name of your school, 'will always be home.' A bunch of people wrote that in my yearbook."

"Tilman's the name of the school," Cynthia said. "But that doesn't seem too appropriate."

Thunk shrugged and grinned at me. I grinned

back. It felt wonderful to be on his side. I couldn't believe Cynthia wasn't writing what he suggested. I mean, *I* would've even if it had been the dumbest thing on earth.

"Maybe you'd like to know that the library is just three streets over," I told him, waving my arm in the general direction of the Villa Verde Library.

Mr. Ambrose waved back.

"It is?" Thunk was gazing at Cynthia and didn't sound too interested.

"There's a shortcut," I said. "You can go along the alley behind Eddie's Market and cross the parking lot of the bakery and that way you can be there in the flick of a lamb's tail."

He didn't answer. "A flick of a lamb's tail is what Mrs. Oda always says," I added, in case he thought I was a total dweeb. "It means fast. I could show you sometime if you like. I live over there." I waved toward my house, and Mr. Ambrose waved back more excitedly than ever. Thunk said nothing. I had the definite feeling I was talking to myself and I was the only one listening.

"They have a chess club at the library," I said in my best peppy voice.

"How about 'Thanks for letting me be Beauty'?" Cynthia asked. The sun turned her hair to gold and struck silver sparks from her belt. She seemed all aglitter. "And maybe 'Good luck with this year's production,' " she added.

"That would be great."

She flashed this dazzling smile. Even her teeth glittered. I ran my tongue over mine, polishing them up.

Thunk turned, and Cynthia propped the program against him while she wrote and while I stood there, shuffling my feet, plucking at the front of my T-shirt to bag it a bit more, not that anyone was noticing. Once in spelling we'd had *unnecessary* . . . two *n*'s, two *s*'s. I knew how to spell it, and from now on I'd never have any trouble putting it in a sentence. Victoria Charlip began to feel unnecessary as she stood in the driveway with Cynthia Sanders and Thunk Shub. One could almost say "invisible." Should I move around to face him, or would that be too obvious? Too obvious. This wasn't working out a bit well.

Then I heard what had to be the most scary sound in the world. Cowboys on scooters, coming fast. I sneaked a look along the sidewalk, and there they were, only half a block away. I never knew scooters could jam like that. Now I could hear Thunk's little brother saying in a loud voice, "It is *not* easier to ride a horse than a camel. Camels have humps."

"Can you hurry, Cynthia?" I asked desperately,

putting my hand up as if to shield my eyes from the sun, but really to hide my face from the little kid who was now right next to us. Fortunately, he was deeply interested in Thunk being a leaning board.

"What are you doing?" he asked.

Thunk sounded impatient. "What does it look like?"

"Where's Mom?" the kid asked.

"I don't know. Inside, I guess."

I turned a little so my back was directly toward the kid.

"C'mon!" The two cowboys were riding off up the driveway, and I let myself slump. Talk about the great escape.

"Here you go," Cynthia said, handing me the program.

I snatched at it, anxious to get out of there, but Thunk got to it first.

"Do they have a play at Fullerton?" he asked, staring down at Cynthia's picture. Fullerton is the junior high they both go to.

"Yes. It's always the same thing every year. The Fullerton Follies."

"Well." I stretched my hand out again, begging for the program.

Cynthia said, "Would you like me to get Tom McCartney to sign it too?" Her finger flicked at the picture of the Beast. Her nails were nice and long, kind of squared off. Of course she wouldn't bite her nails, not Cynthia Sanders. "I'll see him in school tomorrow, and then I could drop the program off at your house after school."

What did she mean after school? Was she planning on walking Thunk home every single day? But I had no time to worry about that now. I had to get out of there.

"That would be nice. Thanks," I said, beginning to edge backward, smiling a nervous smile. It got more nervous when I spotted the two little kids freewheeling back down the driveway from the house. I froze.

"Mom's not there," Thunk's little brother said.

Cynthia smiled at him. "Hi. She's probably around somewhere. Did you try the backyard?"

Uh-oh. The little kid was examining her closely, all squinty-eyed, then turning toward me. I tried not to look at him, but it was like trying not to look at a striking snake. I could tell the very exact second he remembered me.

"Hey! I know who you are," he said. "You're the goofy girl who—"

"Victoria! Victoria!" That was Ellie calling from across the street. Her voice would have wakened the dead, which I just about was. "You have to come!" she yelled. "You have to come now, this second!"

Oh, Ellie, I thought with more gratitude than I'd ever felt for anyone in all my life. Thank you, Ellie.

"Don't forget your pen," Cynthia said.

I turned, flustered, took it, dropped it.

Thunk caught it before it hit the ground. "Here," he said.

"Oh. Thanks, Thunk."

I saw the surprised look on his face and heard the surprise in his voice. "Thanks, *who?*"

"THUNK!" the little kid yelled in a voice as loud as Ellie's. "She thinks you're a terrific hunk. That's why she calls you that."

"It's a case of mistaken identity," I gasped, and then I was running like a rabbit for home and safety.

6

Our two sugar babies lay on the rug in the hallway. I almost stepped on them in my rush to get in the house and close the door behind me.

"Excuse me, Babe. Excuse me, Sweet Sam," I gasped, and got one look at my pale face in the hall mirror before I whispered, "Put me in the closet, Ellie. Lock me up and hide me forever."

Ellie stared at me, big-eyed. "Was it awful, Vicki? Are you OK? Yelling at you to come home was all I could think of."

I nodded. "Thank heaven you did."

It was so silly the way I felt like crying. I collapsed on the floor next to Babe. "It has been such a humiliating day."

Ellie slid down beside me. "When I saw those two little kids coming up the sidewalk, I didn't *know* one of them was Thunk's sneak of a brother. Not till they turned into his driveway." She shook her head in disbelief. "And then they went on toward the house, and I thought you were safe, but then, when they started to come back . . . Are you OK?" she asked again. "Did the little guy remember you?"

I nodded and covered my face with my hands.

Ellie groaned. "Oh, Vicki. I shouldn't have made you go over there. You didn't want to, and I made you."

"You didn't make me. I went by myself."

"So what did the little sneak say?" Ellie asked.

"It wasn't what *he* said, though that was bad enough. It was what *I* said." I told her about "Thanks, Thunk."

Ellie nibbled at her knuckles. "Oh, how awful. Oh, poor you." She fished around in her jeans pocket and brought out a half stick of sugar-free gum. "Here."

"Thanks." I peeled off the rest of the paper and cleaned the fuzz from the broken end.

From behind the closed door of Mom's office came the rat-a-tat of her adding machine, the murmur of voices, and her quick, light laugh.

"Maybe he just thinks you stutter," Ellie said. "Maybe he thought you said, 'Th . . . thanks. Th . . . thanks.' "

"No way. Not after what his kid brother said. I'm finished." I edged along the wall, still sitting, scooped up Babe, and held her in my lap.

"Let's see if they're still out there." Ellie tiptoed back into the living room, and I heard the little rattle of the miniblinds.

"He's gone," she called. "Probably into the house. But Cynthia's heading up the sidewalk on her own. Is that your program she's got?"

"Yes." I was too worn out to explain.

"Maybe Thunk didn't like her that much after all. If he'd liked her, he'd have walked her home, wouldn't he?"

"He liked her." Babe and I joined Ellie at the window.

Cynthia hurried along on the opposite side of the street, her hair bouncing nicely against the back of her neck. Ellie and I have tried to make our hair bounce like that, but there must be a trick to it and it's a trick we don't know. It certainly doesn't work to use spray starch, a tip Tina Fisher told us models use. Tina had definitely been misinformed.

Cynthia was passing the Garcia house. A guy who was cutting the lawn turned his head to watch her pass and rammed his mower into the base of a palm tree. He was a big guy, about eighteen, with fuzz on his bare chest. It certainly says something about Cynthia that a guy with fuzz on his chest is prepared to cut down a palm tree just to watch her pass.

I sighed loudly.

Now she was turning into the Mungers' house, two doors beyond the Garcias.

"What's she going there for?" Ellie asked and answered herself. "Hey, Mr. Munger tutors math. I bet that's what she's doing. I bet that's why she's on our street."

I nodded. "And why she's coming here again tomorrow."

Ellie sniffed. "So now she's making herself smart, too. I swear, some girls are never satisfied. Do you think she likes Thunk?"

"Does a frog like flies? And now that I'm out of the running . . ." Of course, I'd never exactly been *in* the running, but the words sounded sad and satisfying.

There was nothing to see outside now. The street had gone dead except for the fuzzy guy who'd recovered and gone back to mowing the lawn.

Ellie let the miniblind slats close with their little shivery rattle. "I guess I'd better go home. I hate to leave you alone, but—"

"I've got Babe," I said. "I'm going to work on getting her fixed up."

"Try not to think about what happened," Ellie advised.

"I know. I'll try." It was good advice, but I was sure I'd never be able to follow it.

I watched as Ellie and Sweet Sam walked down the street. Ellie's hair did not bounce. The fuzzy guy did not as much as glance in her direction. I felt sad.

My plate with the crumbs of raisin toast was still on the table. "Things weren't so bad when I was eating this," I told Babe, picking her up and hugging her for comfort. "I thought they were, but they weren't. You're all I'm going to think about now. First, you have to have a face. Wait here till I get paper and my marker pens."

I got my ruler, too. Babe was six inches across. I spaced off four inches on the paper, drew a nice oval face, put in big green eyes, a sweet little mouth, two dainty ears, and lots and lots of red curly hair, the kind I'd always wanted myself.

"You're pretty lucky," I told her. "Most kids get stuck with whatever face they get when they're born. You have one custom designed."

I practiced faces over and over before I felt ready to handle the real thing. But drawing on an old pink T-shirt stuffed with sugar wasn't as easy as drawing on paper. Babe looked terrible when I finished, wild-eyed and off-center.

"Uh-oh," I said. "I'm going to have to make your back your front and try again. Turn over on your stomach, Babe." This time I made the outline on the paper pattern thicker and globbed it onto the cloth. The face shape transferred instantly. I deepened the colors. "Now," I said, "you look perfect. And when I get some clothes on you, no one's going to know you have one face in back and another in front. We'll keep your face print. Some babies have footprints. But they're not so interesting."

I carried her to my room and laid her on the bed beside Teddy while I rummaged through my old toy chest. Four years ago my grandma and my aunt Tory, who live in Vienna, Virginia, bought me a Cabbage Patch doll. For the next two Christmases they sent clothes for her, until I suggested she had enough already and that what I'd really like this Christmas was the new book on mummies from the Metropolitan Museum of Art. The Cabbage Patch clothes were still around somewhere. I dragged them out. There was a bright-green polka-dot dress with lace around the collar that fit Babe perfectly. I had to leave the collar unbuttoned in back, since, unfortunately, she'd been born without a neck. I drew legs for her with green buttoned shoes where the feet should be and found a green napkin to drape around her like a cape.

There were sounds of voices and footsteps in the hall now. Mom's clients were leaving. The front door opened and closed, and then Mom called, "Vicki? Vicki? Where are you, hon?"

"In my room." I held Babe up to be admired.

"Wow! Can that be my $2.39 bag of sugar?" Mom asked in mock amazement. "She's perfect— good enough to eat."

"Sh!" I said. "That kind of talk scares her. And she's not *quite* perfect." I pulled the green cotton cape aside to show Mom the crazy-eyed face on the other side. "I messed up."

Mom shivered. "Straight out of the twilight zone."

We smiled at each other, but there was something wrong with the smiles. I could feel mine tight and see Mom's, forced and pale. I knew it was because neither of us had totally forgotten last night's argument. You can't *have* that big an argument and expect everything to be fine the next day.

"But why *can't* I go look after Keiko?" I'd asked.

Mom had been sitting on my bed, and I'd stopped in front of her. "It's not fair. I want to go. They want me. And it'll be real easy, and fun."

"No." I remembered how set Mom's mouth had

been. "I can't imagine what got into your father to even think of such a thing. You're only eleven years old. Suggesting that kind of responsibility is just ridiculous. You taking on the care of a four-year-old for two weeks, entirely on your own—"

"That's not right. You're exaggerating. I wouldn't be entirely on my own. Just during the days. Dad and Yoshi would be there at night and—"

"What if something went wrong one of those days? What would you do? Who would you go to? I would be miles and miles and miles away."

I sighed loudly. "I'd call 911. Or I'd go find an adult in one of the other apartments. There are other people living in the building, you know."

"Oh, that makes me feel a lot better, imagining you running around an apartment house, knocking on the doors of strangers! I'm sorry, Victoria. You are *not* going, so just stop thinking about it. Maybe in a couple of years, when you're older."

"Keiko's my little sister, Mom. OK, my half sister. I love her. I want to get to know her better. Please, please—"

"You can go visit sometime, when your dad and Yoshi are there too."

"I know the real reason you don't want me to go," I'd muttered, turning away, pretending I hadn't wanted her to hear, but making sure she did.

"What does that mean?" Mom had asked quietly.

"Nothing." My hair was still wet from my shower and I grabbed a towel and put it over my head, muttering again. "I know you don't even want me to be *near* him—"

"Take that towel off, Vicki, and listen to me," Mom said in the same quiet voice that's a little scary because there's no way to speak back to it.

I tossed the towel on the bed.

"Last year your father wanted you to go visit them in Waterloo, and I said yes. It was the first approach he'd made to you since he walked out on us nine years ago. I think I might have been forgiven for refusing. He has no legal rights whatsoever. But I thought about you and Keiko, and how you had the same father and you'd never met, and I said yes."

"Big deal," I'd muttered, knowing it was a big deal, the way things were between her and Dad.

"The case is closed," Mom had said. "We're not going to talk about this anymore. I will call your father tomorrow and give him my answer."

Now Mom and I stood here, smiling fake smiles with the memory of yesterday's argument still between us. I wondered if she'd called him yet.

"Did you talk to Dad?" I asked, tracing the outline of Babe's face with the tip of my finger.

"I called. There was no answer. I'll try again to-night."

"Well, look. I'm sorry I was such a snoot and said all those things. I didn't mean them. I was just mad because . . . well, because I really wanted to go." I looked up at her. "I *want* to go—now more than ever."

"Why now more than ever?"

"Well, something awful happened today with the new boy, you know, the one across the street. It was the most embarrassing thing in my whole life, and I'll never get over it. But if I thought I could go away in the summer so we wouldn't have to see each other, it would make it easier. I really, *really*, *really* want to go."

Mom smiled a little, and this time it was a true smile. "I never would have guessed," she said.

I sensed a small weakening and jumped in. "I was thinking. You know this project." I bounced Babe gently up and down. "If I get an A and do really well, that'll mean I'm totally responsible, won't it? And mature?"

"If you're making a comparison here, I'd like to point out there's a small difference between a lively four-year-old and a bag of sugar," Mom said mildly.

"I know that. But Keiko's not that lively, honest. And, I mean, there's no sense in Mrs. Oda making us do this project if it doesn't teach responsibility, right? That's what it's about. And I'm going to be the best in the whole class. The best, Mom."

"Vicki . . ." Mom began.

"Will you please just think about it? Will you put off calling Dad till next Monday, when we get graded? That's all I'm asking. Please, Mom, please."

The tears that had been filling up behind my eyelids spilled over and trickled down my cheeks. Through their blur I could see Mom's surprise. She wasn't half as surprised as I was. Aunt Tory says I cry a lot these days because of my age, whatever that means.

"Honey, there, it's all right." Mom hugged me tight against her. "Don't cry, Vicki."

Babe was squashed between us, and I tried to ease back a bit and give her room without spoiling the moment. Mom held me at arm's length.

"All right. I'll drop your father a note tonight and say that I'm thinking it over and I'll call him next Monday. OK? It doesn't seem quite fair to keep them waiting like this, especially since I can't imagine changing my mind. And I want you to know that, Vicki. I'm postponing this to let you see that I take seriously something that means this much to you. But I don't expect anything to have changed by Monday."

I sniffled a bit and smiled.

"OK, Mom. Thanks."

We hugged again. This time I managed to hold Babe to the side.

We didn't talk anymore about my chances of going to Waterloo while we fixed and ate dinner. I figured it would be better just to keep quiet about it for a while. Afterward, Mom went back in her office and I did my homework and had a shower.

Babe watched me in the dresser mirror as I brushed my wet hair.

"Maybe having a boy know you think he's a Terrific Hunk isn't that bad," I told her. "It might make him notice me, at least. He has to think I have good taste." I stopped brushing and brooded at my reflection. That argument didn't make a lot of sense, somehow. "Rats," I said. "Forget about it, OK?" And I was trying to, fixing an old Easter basket to be a bed for Babe, when the phone rang.

We have three phones, one in the kitchen and one in Mom's bedroom. The third has a separate number and is in Mom's office. I know their different sounds. This was the one that rings in the kitchen and bedroom.

I heard Mom's office door open, her footsteps going to the kitchen, the murmur of her voice.

"Vicki? It's for you," she called from the bottom of the stairs.

"Is it Ellie?" Ellie and I aren't allowed to phone each other this late, but sometimes, in emergencies, we break the rules. She was probably worrying about me.

"It isn't Ellie." Mom lowered her voice as I came partway down the stairs. "It's a boy."

"A boy? For me?" I could hardly breathe as I checked that my ears were in place. "Wait . . . tell him to wait just a second. I have to get Babe."

A boy? The only boy who ever calls me is my cousin Salvo, and that's only because my aunt Tory makes him call every year on my birthday.

"This isn't my birthday, is it?" I whispered to Mom as she gave me the phone.

"No," she said.

Then this was definitely not my cousin Salvo.

I took another few seconds to stop snorting before I picked up the phone.

7

"Hello?" the boy on the phone said.

I couldn't seem to answer. What was the matter with my throat, anyway?

"Hello?" he said again.

This was a *boy*? How had Mom known? The voice was high and trembling. Immediately I knew it couldn't be Thunk—not with a Donald Duck squeak like this.

"This is Vicki Charlip," I said.

There was silence, and then I heard "This is Vicki Charlip" repeated in that sneery, drive-me-crazy way.

"I think there's an echo on the phone," I said coldly. "What do you want, Harry Hogan?"

"What page is our math homework?" he asked.

"You called me for *that*?" I scowled at the phone. "How come you're calling me? It's way after ten. How come you haven't done your homework by now?"

"Because I had some other stuff to do," he said. "Some important stuff."

I sniffed. "I'm sure. The math's page fifty-four. And it's *hard*." I hung up the phone and turned to Mom, who was looking through the ad section of the newspaper and pretending not to listen. "It wasn't a boy," I told her. "It was just Harry Hogan."

Mom smiled. "Poor thing! He sounded nervous." I didn't feel a bit like smiling. My first phone call from a boy, if you wanted to call him a boy, and it had to be Horrible Harry Hogan.

"Does that have to count as the thrill of a lifetime?" I asked Ellie as we walked to school the next morning.

Ellie looked sympathetic.

She and I'd read an article in *Cute* that listed a girl's first phone call from a boy along with the first kiss as the thrills of a lifetime. "You'll still recall it vividly when you're old and gray," the article said.

"Imagine," I said. "Being old and gray and having to think about Horrible Harry Hogan."

We swung our baskets with our sugar babies in them as we walked. Ellie's mom had given her a wicker sewing box that was missing its lid. Ellie said there were no old Easter baskets in their house because they got retrimmed and passed down from kid to kid, which was one of the many disadvantages of a large family.

I stopped to rearrange the pillow of pink Kleenex under Babe's head.

"Do you really like the way I've fixed Sweet Sam up to be Superman?" Ellie asked for the tenth time.

And I said, "I really do. It's perfectly magical how he changed overnight."

Ellie had painted him bright blue with a big yellow S on his chest, and had dressed him in a red cape and those crazy red shorts over his leotards.

"I wonder how come Superman wears his underwear outside," I asked. "It's so weird."

Ellie patted Sweet Sam protectively. "I think it looks good."

"Imagine if the boys in Mrs. Oda's class began doing that?" I asked, and Ellie said, "Oh, gross! Pudgy Jeremiah Green!" and we began giggling and nudging each other with our elbows.

"Uh-oh," Ellie warned. "Careful! Bicycle coming."

We checked over our shoulders, poised for immediate action, but it was only a girl in a denim jumpsuit and not Thunk cycling behind us, so we relaxed. We'd already planned that if Thunk did appear, we'd stash our babies behind the nearest wall or shrubbery, quick as the flick of a lamb's tail. I'd taken the added precaution of wearing my bent old tennis hat that sags on both sides and my shocking-pink, heart-shaped sunglasses.

As soon as the girl passed, we checked the street behind.

"All clear," Ellie said.

"I guess I'm in these glasses and this hat all year, till Thunk leaves," I muttered. "But at least the hat's good for disguising ears. Not that he'd know me anyway. Not that he'd *want* to," I added.

"Oh, he *would*," Ellie said, much too cheerfully.

We were at the gates of Tilman, so I stuffed my hat and glasses into my backpack. We were safe inside. Was that Horrible Harry Hogan's voice booming along the corridor from Mrs. Oda's room?

"What's he saying?" Ellie cupped one hand behind her ear and screwed up her face. Now we could hear.

"You have a lovely, sweet-looking neck, my dear. Just right for my kiss of death."

Now we were at the room and we could see the crush of kids around Harry Hogan's desk. Judy Petrone was shrieking and holding her sugar baby high above her head, while Harry Hogan raced behind her holding his sugar baby high too.

"Good grief," Ellie gasped. "What has he done?"

Harry Hogan's baby was painted black with a white tuxedo front. Its hair was slick and shiny paint, black as licorice, and underneath was this chalk-white face with an awful red mouth. Little drops of red trickled from the corners.

"Blood!" I said.

Horrible Harry made the thing zoom in my direction, heading right for Babe.

"Stop that, Harry Hogan!" I yelled.

"Nuzzing can save you," Harry whispered, and then Ellie said, "Toom to toom toom. . . . Stand back! Superman to the rescue!"

We were all screaming and shoving and stamping around the room when Mrs. Oda came in.

"Oh, my," she said in her calm smiling voice. "Am I in the wrong room? I thought this was a class to teach responsibility."

"Dracula's after Babe," I gasped.

"And all of our babies," Tina Fisher added. I saw that she had one hand on each twin. They lay side by side in a little red wagon beside her desk. What a good idea when you have two to lug around, I thought.

Mrs. Oda took everything in at a glance.

"Put Count Dracula back in his coffin, Harry," she said. "He can't be out in daylight anyway. You know that."

I'd been too busy protecting Babe to notice any coffin, but now I saw the huge black-painted shoe box on Harry Hogan's desk. On the side I could faintly see Size 15D, Cordova Brown Cowboy Boots. Who was big enough to wear size fifteens? Harry's Dad? King Kong?

Mrs. Oda beamed around the room. I'd never seen her look so pleased.

"I can tell that all of you have put a big effort into this. Why don't each of you introduce your sugar babies to the class? We'll start with Victoria."

"This is Babe," I said proudly.

Mrs. Oda smiled. "My goodness! Real clothes!"

"She has a whole wardrobe of things," I bragged. "She can have a new outfit every day."

"And I vill pay her a visit this very night," Harry Hogan whispered behind me. I wiped my hair where his voice had touched. "Stop it, Harry Hogan."

"Harry can't show his masterpiece because of the power of sunlight," Mrs. Oda said. "But I think you've all met Count Dracula."

I could hardly believe what great-looking sugar babies we had. Mrs. Oda had brought her camera so we could have a class picture, and we posed in front of the blackboard. Then she carefully took a picture of each baby and recorded the names. We had Princess Di and Miss Dolly and Pelé, which is

70

pronounced Pay Lay and is the name of a famous soccer player who is George Cuesta's hero. "He doesn't play anymore, but he's still superior," George said.

Tina Fisher called her twins C and H.

"That's what it said on their stomachs," Tina said. "And it's fine with me."

"You sound pretty tired, Tina," Mrs. Oda said.

Tina nodded. "Twins wear you out."

She sounded so important and different and know-it-all that for a minute I almost wished *I'd* been the one to get the twins. But maybe not.

Barbara Sandberg had made cards which she passed out.

BARBARA'S SITTING SERVICE
I will watch your babies during
recess and lunch.
Twenty-five cents a day.
Guaranteed.

"Guaranteed by what?" Horrible Harry Hogan asked. "You got references? I'm not leaving Drac with you. No way."

"I wouldn't take him," Barbara said. "He's gross-out city."

But Harry did leave Dracula at lunch. Almost all the kids left their babies, and Barbara took IOUs from anyone who didn't have a quarter. It was pretty funny. There was Barbara, under the oak tree, surrounded by snoopy little fourth and fifth graders, and Barbara saying, "No, you can't hold one of them. I am responsible here. These are babies, not toys."

Ellie and I walked Babe and Sweet Sam/Superman inside the fence while the others played soccer or handball or whatever.

"You can't be too careful," we told each other smugly.

"I have an idea for you with your mom," Ellie said after a while.

"Really?!"

"Why don't you get Keiko to call and ask if you can go stay with her. Moms can never resist little kids. The ones in our house are spoiled rotten."

"It might work. Keiko is pretty irresistible." I smiled, thinking about her shiny black hair, her little stick legs, the way she uses big, serious words, like "fragile," that sound so funny coming from a little kid. "My dolly's fragile, Vicki." But it was sad, too. I wished she wasn't so far away. I wished the two of us could live together and be real sisters.

Later in the afternoon Mrs. Oda had us draw our family trees, and I penciled Keiko in beside me on the branch that came down from Dad and Mom, and Babe on a branch that came down from me.

"Keiko! What a pretty name," Mrs. Oda said. "I didn't know you had a little sister, Victoria."

"She's four," I said, and I used my red pencil to draw a heart next to her name.

Babe and I had to walk home alone after school because Ellie's mom was picking up her and Sweet Sam/Superman to go to the mall. Their station wagon was overflowing with kids, as usual, all of them hanging out the windows, shouting to me about my neat pink glasses and how cute Babe was, waving toys, punching each other, laughing and howling. I've never seen their station wagon without a baby car seat. There used to be two. Ellie's family always seems to be having so much fun, even when they're squabbling. Today I could have sworn there were more kids than usual. I think there were some there that didn't even belong in their family. It made me feel sad and lonely as Babe and I walked home alone. Being an only child has nice things going for it, I guess. Sometimes Ellie says she envies me, even, because I get all the attention from my mom and she hardly gets any, which isn't true. But I'm the one who envies her. She has all those brothers and sisters to love her. I'm sure they do, even though it's hard to tell sometimes. If Mom and Dad had stayed together I might have had brothers and sisters too, instead of being stuck with being an "only." But actually, I have Keiko. And if all goes well, this might be the beginning of lots and lots of visits.

I walked faster. No need to worry about Thunk seeing me. Junior high doesn't let out till an hour after we do. His twerpy little brother might be around, but surely I could handle a twerpy little preschooler. Not that I'd done such a world-class job yesterday.

Mr. Ambrose waved happily as I turned the corner into our street. I'm not sure if he recognized me behind my glasses and under my hat or if he was just doing his usual thing. I waved back.

Before I stopped to talk to him, I checked carefully behind Ophelia's bushes for eavesdroppers. Nobody there.

E-a-v-e-s-d-r-o-p-p-e-r. Someone who listens in on private conversations.

Across the street Thunk's house slept in the sun. A trickle of water darkened the hot driveway and a few dried-up magnolia leaves curled like question marks on the boulevard grass. Someone had placed two clay pots of scarlet geraniums by the front door. Would Thunk and Cynthia Sanders walk home from school together today? Would she remember to bring the play program, maybe even bring it across to my house? Would Thunk say, "Oh, that's right, that weird girl, the one with the funny ears, asked you to . . ."

I swallowed hard and blinked up at Mr. Ambrose.

"Do you like the way I've fixed up my baby?" I asked. One good thing about Mr. Ambrose, he wouldn't notice that my voice was wobbly. I lifted one side of my pink heart glasses with my finger so he could see. "It's Vicki," I said.

Mr. Ambrose smiled his delight. "No clouds on the mountain," he said, pointing. "No storm in sight."

"I think you're right," I told him. "Listen, you know I told you about Mom not wanting me to go to Iowa? Well, Ellie has this idea about getting Keiko to—"

There was a whirr of bicycle wheels across the street. My head jerked almost the whole way around, like the little girl in *The Exorcist.*

And there was Thunk cycling down his driveway. He was talking over his shoulder to someone, and I knew he hadn't spotted us yet. But he couldn't miss us. For one thing, Mr. Ambrose was poised to wave and there would be no stopping him.

What could I do? What?

Quick as a flick I popped Babe, basket and all,

behind the trunk of the big palm tree on the boulevard just the way Ellie and I had planned. I wished I could have popped me behind it too.

Now Thunk saw us. But I was sure he hadn't seen Babe.

"Hi, Vicki," he called.

Good heavens! He remembered my name! He knew me even in my disguise!

"Er, hi." I checked my ears, but they were mercifully in control under the hat.

Oh, heavens. He was stopping. I took a step forward, leaning nonchalantly against the palm. "Aren't you out early?" I asked.

He nodded. "Half day. Do you have a bike?"

"A bike?" I took a raggedy breath and nodded.

"Want to get it and show me that fast way to the library?"

My heart was jumping in a skittery sort of way.

"Sure," I said. "I'll get it."

Thunk rode beside me as I walked quickly away. What if Mr. Ambrose called, "Hey, Vicki. You forgot your sugar baby."

He wouldn't, though.

You could leave a brontosaurus behind the palm tree and Mr. Ambrose would just keep on smiling and waving.

I didn't even say good-bye to him as I rushed

away, hurrying in case Thunk would change his mind.

But I did glance back once at Babe, lying there, abandoned in her Easter basket.

8

A long, white Lincoln Continental that must belong to one of Mom's clients was parked in our driveway. Mom kidded that it was clients like that who brought a touch of class to our neighborhood. I got my bike from the garage and maneuvered it out.

Thunk waited by our side patio and I sensed his impatience, so I hurried like crazy.

"Ready," I gasped, an astronaut two seconds before blast-off.

Thunk was looking seriously gorgeous. He was wearing khaki shorts and a jeans jacket with the sleeves cut out so the armholes were nice and raggedy. The jacket buttons were all open in a very macho way, and he had his yellow plastic bike chain over one shoulder and across his chest, like a bandit's belt of bullets. If I was going to be picky, I'd have said that his shorts were a bit long and droopy. Otherwise he was perfect.

"Let's go," he said.

I rode closest to the curb, making sure I was between him and any sight of Babe.

As we passed Ophelia's house, we saw her backing her car out of their driveway. Her father waved her off, probably to the grocery store. She used to take him with her, but he got in the way of the shoppers, standing in the aisles giving out weather forecasts, so now she left him home. But never for long.

Thunk and I sped past, getting our share of waves. I told myself I wouldn't look back for a last glimpse of Babe, but I did. All I could see was the basket handle and the pale curve of the wicker side. That was enough to make me feel awful.

What was I doing? This wasn't right. I shouldn't be leaving her like this. In the first place, I was on my honor, and in the second place, what kind of mother would forsake her child?

"Are you coming or what?" Thunk called impatiently. He was already three houses ahead.

"Just a sec," I yelled. "I have to tell Mr. Ambrose something."

As far away as he was, I could still see that Thunk was getting mad. Probably when you looked the way he looked, girls didn't keep you waiting. He was muttering something and tossing his head in a can-you-believe-it? kind of way, but I couldn't hear, which was just as well.

I swung back to Mr. Ambrose. "Look," I whispered. "That's my baby there in the basket." I glanced quickly at Thunk and then risked pointing at Babe. "See her? Will you look after her till I get back?"

Mr. Ambrose shuffled uncertainly and rubbed his hands together.

"Could be warm tomorrow," he said. "Seventy-five degrees wouldn't surprise me. No, sir. I guess it might make it to seventy-five."

"I got to go, Vicki," Thunk called. "See you."

"Wait! I'm coming!" and to Mr. Ambrose I said one last time, "Look after her."

Thunk was zigzagging back and forth across the street.

"I'm in a hurry, you know," he said as I puffed up beside him.

"I know. I'm sorry. But that was important." To show how apologetic I was, I pedaled furiously, getting ahead of him, calling, "This way. Cross over here." I roared us through the alley behind Eddie's Market, across the bakery parking lot, under the awning of the pizza parlor and the photography shop, and all the time I was thinking, can this be real? Thunk and I? It was like a dream come true. It was definitely the thrill of a lifetime, whether *Cute* listed it or not. I could have ridden beside him all the way to China, but that was not where we were going.

"We're here," I said triumphantly.

Our library is very pretty, a peaceful island of shady lawns and trees right in the middle of all that traffic. There's an outside patio where doves coo and where hummingbirds come to drink from a bottle of bright-red nectar. About once every two years there are rumblings that the library's going to be knocked down and a mini-mall put up in its place. Then a whole bunch of us—Mrs. Coles and Mrs. Ting from our street and the Sobels, who own Thunk's house, and scads of students from the college—take petitions around. We picket, too. Mom and I have carried so many signs that say SAVE OUR LIBRARY that I feel I partly own it, I've saved it now so many times.

"It's nice, isn't it?" I asked Thunk. "See the carvings above the door? A really famous artist designed those. His name was Mr. Dolittle, but he did a lot."

"Really!" Thunk said. I was glad he at least took time to look.

The Mitchells' dog was sleeping by the bike rack in front, and he opened his eyes and waved his tail at us. The Mitchells have a very free-traveling dog.

He has picketed with us a couple of times, so he probably thinks he owns the library too. Thunk parked his bike and I parked mine beside it. He whipped his chain from around his chest.

"Maybe you could lock both bikes together," I suggested.

Thunk looked surprised. "Are you coming in?"

"Well, sure." What had he expected? That I'd lead him here like an Indian Scout and slink away into the sunset?

"I'm going to be a while," he said, frowning.

I thought fleetingly of Babe and of the fact that I hadn't even left Mom a gone-to-the-library note. But both thoughts came and went quickly.

"That's OK," I said. "I have stuff to do too."

Maybe I could call Mom from the phone around back. And I'd ask her if she could go get Babe. Wait. She'd think I hadn't been very responsible leaving my sugar baby there. She might even say, "What happened to your word of honor?" or "So that's the way you plan on looking after Keiko, is it? Remember, there'll be no mom in Iowa when you get yourself into a mess." That was silly, of course. I'd never leave Keiko behind a palm tree. But still. Better not call. Mom had that Lincoln Continental person there anyway. And she might not notice I wasn't home.

I stared down at Thunk, who was putting the yellow chain around our wheels. The beginnings of his nice shoulders were daringly revealed by the sleeveless jeans jacket. I decided Ellie had picked the perfect name for him. Some Terrific Hunk. I fixed my hat, running my finger around the brim to check that one of my ears hadn't popped out. My ears will do that.

"OK." Thunk straightened and gave me that nice, toothy smile. He had a new little bump on his chin, but it didn't look that bad.

"OK," I said, smiling pretty toothily myself.

The inside of the library was dim and smelled sweet, like bubble gum. In the hopes that there'd be some kids from Tilman here, I removed my glasses so I could see and also be seen, with Thunk.

And the first person I saw was Cynthia Sanders. The second was Horrible Harry Hogan. They were at the same table, even, along with a woman with corkscrew hair and hoop earrings big enough for a tiger to jump through.

Thunk was heading for the only empty chair at the table.

"Hi, Cynthia," he said, plopping himself down. "Sorry I'm late."

Late? Oh, no, he'd been coming to meet her! That's why he'd been in such a hurry. I *had* been just an Indian Scout. All at once I felt as droopy as Thunk's shorts.

Horrible Harry Hogan looked up, of course. So did Cynthia, who said, "Hi, Sam. Hi, Vicki. Oh, shoot! I got your *Beauty and the Beast* program signed, but I left it in my locker. Sorry."

Sam? Thunk was Sam?

"That's OK," I told Cynthia. "Thanks."

Sam Shub. It had a great sound. But I knew that nevertheless Sam would be Thunk to me forever.

"What *Beauty and the Beast* program?" Horrible Harry Hogan asked with interest.

"Last year's."

"What do you want last year's program for?" he asked.

"Something," I said.

"Something," he repeated. I could have bopped him. Weren't things bad enough? Why did *he* have to be here?

"Don't do that to Vicki," Cynthia Sanders told him. "Echoing like that drives people crazy. The last time I heard you do that was to Linda Gonzales, and we both know why." She nudged Harry Hogan and made little kissing sounds.

"Quit it, Cynthia." Harry Hogan gave Cynthia a nudge back and shot me a nervous look. I couldn't figure what was going on. And I especially couldn't figure how Cynthia and Harry Hogan seemed to be on such friendly nudging terms.

"Do you want me to tell Vicki why you teased Linda?" Cynthia asked.

"You do that and you're in deep yogurt," Harry Hogan said, and they grinned and nudged each other again.

I tried to keep my mouth from dropping open. Horrible Harry Hogan and beautiful Cynthia Sanders had kidding conversations? It was beyond belief.

"I didn't know you and Harry Hogan were . . . eh, friends, Cynthia," I said.

"Sure. We live next door to each other."

"Worse luck," Horrible Harry added. Now he was looking carefully at me. "Where's Babe?"

"Oh, I left her with someone," I said.

"Your mom?"

I noticed that the black boot box, size 15D, that was Dracula's bed was parked on the floor beside Horrible Harry's chair, lid tightly in place.

"No, not with my mom," I said. "With a neighbor. Sort of a grandfather person."

I was afraid to look at Thunk in case he'd ask, "*Who* did you leave?" and I'd have to explain about sugar babies after all, but he didn't ask. He was too absorbed with Cynthia.

"We're doing a report together, Sam and I," Cynthia said, and then added, "Hey, maybe Vicki wanted to sit there. You took the only seat, Sam."

The woman with the corkscrew hair said, "I can move if the four of you want to sit together," but I quickly said, "Thanks, but it's OK. I have to look for a book. I'm not staying. See you guys."

I went at top speed to the nearest bookshelves and got myself behind them.

How awful! Imagine, sitting with the three of them! And I'd been so dumb to think Thunk wanted to go somewhere with me. Had I looked really jazzed about it? Had I looked like a dweeb?

I peered around the edge of the bookshelves and saw him bestowing this dazzle of a smile on Cynthia. How could she just sit there? If Thunk looked at me like that, I'd be jumping up and down. But if Cynthia jumped up and down for every boy who looked at her, she'd be exhausted. And for *this* I'd left Babe! My eyes felt weird and I fished my glasses out of my pocket and put them on. Well, I'd just sneak out now and disappear, maybe forever—except my bike was hooked to Thunk's. So? I'd go back and say, "OK. I got the information I came for. Can you unhook my bike, please, Thunk . . . er, I mean, Sam."

There was a fat red book at eye level. I pulled it off the shelf, opened a page, and read, "It is just

two hundred years ago that Newton closed his eyes."
The author was Einstein, so that ought to be all
right. I shelved the book again in its space, glued
on a smile, and walked back to the table. Thunk
and Cynthia leaned over her notebook. Horrible
Harry Hogan was writing in our spelling workbook,
probably doing his homework. The lady seemed to
be copying down a recipe from a magazine. The
tip of her tongue was stuck out between her lips.
None of them looked up, and I had to give a little
cough.

"Cool sunglasses," Harry Hogan said at once.

"Yeah, well," I tapped the edge of the table.
"I'm sorry to interrupt you . . . er . . . Sam. But
I need to get my bike."

"Your bike?" He didn't even remember *that* much
about us.

"It's locked with yours," I said. "I'm ready to
go. I got the information about Newton."

"Already?" Cynthia sounded amazed. "That was
fast." Today she was wearing a white tunic thing
and white leggings. If she'd had a turban, she could
have been one of those religious people. But I had
to admit she looked really superior.

"It was just two hundred years ago that Newton
closed his eyes," I said. My glasses were slipping,
probably because I'd gone all sweaty. I pushed them

back up. Oh, how I wished Ellie were here. Ellie would have helped me get through this.

"Was Newton the guy who slept so long and when he woke up, everything had changed?" Harry Hogan asked.

"That was Rip Van Winkle, you zombo," Cynthia told him.

"So, can I get my bike?" I asked Thunk.

"Sure."

I started for the door. "You better take good care of Babe," Harry Hogan called after me, and I almost died. Had he guessed? He couldn't have.

"Don't forget to guard the doors and windows after sunset," he called. "The Count is coming," and I realized he was just warning me about Dracula. Thank goodness.

Thunk and I were both hurrying over the sun-warmed grass now, Thunk probably desperate to get back to Cynthia, me to get away from here, to get back to Babe.

The Mitchells' dog still dozed in the sun. This time he didn't even open his eyes. They stayed closed tight as Newton's.

Thunk unchained our bikes. I thought separating them like that was probably symbolic, but I hadn't time to think about it now.

"There you go." He gave me that smile, but it

wasn't the same as the one he gave Cynthia. He wasn't really behind this one.

"Thanks," I said, and I was gone, cycling fast as I could under the awnings, through the parking lot, along the alley at the back of Eddie's Market.

There's a mailbox on our corner, and Thunk's little brother and the Garcia kid were hiding on the other side of it. They both had water pistols now, and they leaped in my direction, squirting furiously. Fortunately, I saw them coming and veered out of range. The streams missed me by inches.

"You're goofy-looking in that hat and stuff," the little twerp yelled.

"Goofy-looking yourself," I yelled back, standing straight on the pedals so I could see down our tree-shadowed street.

Oh, good, there was Mr. Ambrose, exactly where I'd left him. Ophelia's car wasn't in their driveway, so I couldn't have been gone that long . . . twenty-five minutes or so. Mr. Ambrose waved and I waved back. I couldn't see the basket yet, but I was still pretty far away.

Closer.

Closer.

Now I could see perfectly.

I could see that the basket was gone.

9

I threw my bike on the boulevard and ran around to the back of the palm tree. All I saw was flattened long grass, the snuggle nest where my basket had been, but wasn't now.

Mr. Ambrose paid no attention to me. He was busy waving to Mrs. Coles and Mrs. Ting, who were out for their afternoon walk, striding by on the opposite sidewalk.

I tugged at his sleeve to get his attention. "Where's my sugar baby?"

He blinked nervously at me and the smile quivered.

"Going to be nice tomorrow," he said. "Having a spell of sunshine. Yes, sir."

I changed my grip to his arm. "Did you move Babe? Where is she?"

"Seventy-five degrees," he said. "I wouldn't be surprised."

Oh, criminy! If only he could tell me. Maybe he'd taken Babe inside. Sure. He probably had.

Ophelia's door is always open so her father can go in and out when he wants to. I ran up the path and leaped the three steps to the porch. "I'm going inside, OK?" I called back to Mr. Ambrose.

He had his back to me, watching a Merry Plumbers truck that had pulled to a stop across the street, in front of Thunk's house.

I pushed open the door. The living room was cool and shady, smelling of the roses from Ophelia's garden. A bowl of them spilled petals on the top of the piano.

No sugar baby here. Should I go through and check out the bedrooms? I couldn't. That would be too nervy. I'd have to wait till Ophelia came home and ask her, but already I had this horrible, empty feeling. Babe was gone.

I came slowly back down the path. Ophelia's ginger cat, Stumpy, came from under a bush to hiss at me and glare with yellow eyes. Stumpy and I dislike each other and usually I hiss back, but today I didn't have the strength.

I ran up to the mailbox, where Thunk's little brother and his friend still lay in ambush.

"Did either of you two guys take a basket I left behind the palm tree?"

"A basket?" The Garcia kid wrinkled his face in disgust. "Baskets are for girls."

Thunk's little brother spread his legs apart and stared up at me. "Where'd you get those funky glasses anyway?"

"Never mind," I said.

He examined his water pistol and then me with a crafty look, and I knew he was just about to unload the rest of the water right into my face. "If you shoot that thing at me, you're dead meat," I warned.

They hadn't taken Babe. I could tell.

Slowly I walked back, checking behind every bush and every piece of shrubbery. I kicked through ivy, trailed a searching hand through iceplant. There was no basket anywhere.

And all the time thoughts mushed around inside my head. I'd have to go home and tell Mom what I'd done.

"I can't believe you just went off like that and left Babe behind," she'd say. "Weren't you on your honor to take her with you everywhere you went? I don't *care* that it was because the cute new boy from across the street asked you to go with him to the library. What kind of reason is that? Don't talk to me about responsibility, Victoria."

And tomorrow I'd be the only childless parent in Mrs. Oda's class. I'd have to confess. And I'd get an F. My first F ever. Mrs. Oda wouldn't say she was disappointed in me, but I'd know. And Horrible Harry Hogan would give that hyena laugh of his. "Miss Goody-Goody Victoria Charlip. Oh, wow! I thought you said you left her with your *grandfather*."

Keiko . . . Iowa . . . everything drifted slowly in front of my eyes. No hope now. All gone.

And why was I walking along here anyway, checking out people's yards? Who'd take Babe and move her? It didn't make sense.

I peered through a crack in the fence of the corner house where the minister and his wife live. Their neat, no-nonsense yard was empty. No Babe. Of course not.

I leaned against the sun-warmed fence for a minute. Maybe I should put a lost-and-found notice on every tree. I'd offer a reward. But if I put up notices, everyone would know I'd lost Babe.

Mr. Ambrose saw me coming and waved frantically, as if he hadn't laid eyes on me for a month at least. I decided to try asking him one more time. "Listen . . . did you see somebody take—"

"Warm for March," he said. "Going to get warmer, too."

For the first time ever, I wanted to shake him. "My baby's lost and it's *your* fault. You didn't take care of her properly." I'd left Babe in his care for what? A half hour? He was a grown man, for heaven's sake. Wouldn't you think . . . ?

Mr. Ambrose's face twisted up. Beads of perspiration gleamed on his forehead. "It's . . . I think it might storm," he said, stammering a bit, his chin still moving up and down when the words stopped.

And then I stood there, feeling lost myself. Lost and rotten. "I'm sorry," I began.

I grabbed ahold of his hand. "Oh, Mr. Ambrose. I'm sorry. It was nobody's fault but mine. I thought maybe Thunk liked me, and that was why he wanted me to go with him, but, of course, he didn't. He likes Cynthia Sanders. She's so pretty. Beautiful. Not much wonder he likes her."

Mr. Ambrose stared over my head. I'd hurt him a lot. I could tell. He was my best grown-up friend, and I'd said all those horrible things.

An AT&T telephone van came rattling down the street, and Mr. Ambrose turned. I thought he was getting set to wave, but he didn't. Instead, he took off his glasses, rubbed them across the front of his shirt, put them on again. His shoulders sagged.

And then I saw Ophelia's station wagon making

the turn at the end of the block. I'd wait and ask her if she knew anything about Babe. But how would she know? She'd been gone. Anyway, I didn't want to face her after being so mean to her father.

I picked up my bike and headed for home.

Inside I could hear the hum of voices coming from Mom's office. I tiptoed past and ran upstairs. The little red lacquered box on my dresser had seven dollars and thirty-five cents in it. I think I was just checking to see how big a reward I could offer. I think that's what I was doing. Instead, I took three dollars and ran back downstairs.

Even as I wrote the note to leave on the kitchen table for Mom, I wasn't sure what I was going to do. I don't think I was sure. But why was I slipping out, then, getting on my bike and taking off again?

Usually I can ride to Gertmenian's Market in ten minutes. It took me longer today because I went the long way around, even doubling back one block. Maybe I needed time to make up my mind. Or change it. Maybe I was afraid I'd be seen. I couldn't seem to decide why I was doing anything.

Mr. Gertmenian knows me and Mom well. His little market is so close we go there a lot. Actually, Eddie's up by the library is closer, but I wasn't going back that way again. Today Mr. Gertmenian's shades were drawn against the sun and one of the placards on the window had fallen down so it hung by one corner. AVOCADOS 4 FOR A DOLLAR.

Inside, Mr. Gertmenian, fat and white-aproned, leaned behind the counter reading the sports section of the *Star News.*

"Hello, Tricky Vicki," he said.

Oh, no! I almost stopped breathing. What did he know? Did he suspect?

And then I remembered: Mr. Gertmenian calls me Tricky Vicki sometimes because it rhymes. Ellie said she told him her name was Eleanor when he asked because there are too many awful words that rhyme with Ellie. She didn't want to get him started.

It's funny. I'd never thought much about Tricky Vicki before. But I was thinking about it now as I checked out all the aisles in case someone from Tilman might be here. But there was only a lady with a little girl who was whining for gum or licorice or a Popsicle and saying over and over "I want . . . I want . . ."

For some reason I was saying it too. "I want . . . I want. . . ."

Here was the shelf.

I pulled my hat lower over my sunglasses before I picked out a five-pound bag of sugar and carried it to the cash register.

10

The Lincoln Continental was gone from our driveway. In its place was a Honda Accord with roof racks and a bumper sticker that said, I'D RATHER BE SURFING. Some of Mom's clients are more interesting than others.

I slipped past the office door, got Mom's sewing box and the rest of the faded camp T-shirt that I'd shoved back in the ragbag, and tiptoed upstairs.

By the time I heard our front door open and close and Mom calling, " 'Bye, Jon," I had Babe II sewn into her new skin and I'd used the face pattern and my crayons to change her into a person. When Mom came up into my room, I was crouched by my toy box searching for the rest of the Cabbage Patch doll clothes.

"Well!" Mom gave Babe no more than a passing glance. "I see your child is getting a new outfit."

"Yep." I pulled a little yellow skirt and a green vest with yellow flowers out from the toy chest.

"There's a yellow blouse to go under this somewhere, but since she doesn't have arms, I don't think I'll bother."

For some reason it was hard for me to look at Mom. But I could tell she was looking at me.

"Vicki, honey? Do you feel all right? You're flushed." She came across and put her hand against my cheek, her voice so soft and loving I wanted to bawl. She was being nice to me, and I was such a cheat.

"I'm OK."

I jerked my head away, stood, and walked to my dresser. I'd left the lid off my little red money box, and I set it back on. In the mirror I saw myself, still wearing the stupid hat. Had I always had such small, shifty eyes?

Mom sat on my bed and patted the place beside her. "Come sit for a minute, love. I want to talk to you."

My heart did that little pause thing, then raced ahead of itself. What did she want? I looked quickly at Babe and away. There was no difference, was there? Mom couldn't know. Awful to feel so guilty.

I sat carefully beside her, smoothing the yellow Cabbage Patch doll skirt across my knees, looking at it with great concentration.

"Your father called," Mom said.

"Oh."

"He wanted to know if I'd made a decision yet, about letting you go to take care of Keiko. I told him not yet. I told him I'd promised you that I'd think about it. I said I'd let him know on Monday."

I was smoothing and smoothing the doll skirt. It was terribly wrinkled. Maybe I'd have to iron it. It was so little, though, wouldn't it be hard to iron? Would it fit over the board?

"I explained to him about Babe, and how you said if you did a good job with *her*, it should qualify you for Keiko." Mom smiled, but I couldn't make myself smile back. "Your dad said he was sure you'd do a good job." She paused. "I told him that he should line up someone else, just in case I don't change my mind." Her hand covered mine. "Can you understand my thinking on this, Vicki? My worry for you. You're just a little girl yourself."

I nodded. "I understand."

"You do?" Mom sounded surprised and pleased. After all the things I'd said, she must be wondering why I was so reasonable now. "I'm glad. However . . ." She leaned over and picked up Babe II. "We'll still keep the discussion lines open, you and I. That's a promise. Your father says that every night Keiko asks when you're coming. So I know seeing you again means a lot to her, too. Maybe I shouldn't have told you that. I just wanted you to know that the love is there on her side, too."

"I'm glad you told me." I lifted my head for the first time and stared out the window, thinking about Keiko in her little bed, the butterfly mobile above her head turning in drifts of orange and yellow. Dad had made it for her, painting the butterflies, real in every detail. He would have finished reading her "Goldilocks," the way he did every night and . . . I blinked.

"Did Dad read to me when I was little, Mom?"

Mom nodded. "He was a nice father, in his way. He was just too young, Vicki, not ready to be married, certainly not ready to have a baby. We were both too young." She ran her hand across Babe II. "You can see, yourself, just a little, how hard it is to be on duty with a baby twenty-four hours a day."

I bit my lip. If she only knew!

"So Dad just took off?" I asked quickly.

"Vicki, there are people who are so good at what they do, so anxious to do it better, so . . . obsessed, that they resent any other demands on their time or their lives. Your father was like that about his painting."

"But he got married again. And they had Keiko."

Mom smiled. "He's older. He probably found out that even geniuses get lonely."

"Do you think Dad's a genius, Mom?"

"Not really. And I think he found that out, too. It was probably very hard for him."

"Well, when he discovered all those things, that he was lonely and wasn't a genius, why didn't he come back to us? We were here."

"Oh, honey!" Mom leaned forward and laid her cheek against my hair. "Edges don't fit together that way, or hardly ever. Life is too complicated. For one thing, he found Yoshi. She shares his interests. And I'm glad he didn't come back to us. I've changed, too. I wouldn't have wanted him. I'm sorry, honey, but that's the truth." She kissed my forehead. "But I've always, always wanted you."

And then my heart began racing again. Mom was holding Babe on her lap, and I realized I'd forgotten that the original Babe had a face on the back of her head as well as on the front. *This* Babe hadn't. Any second now Mom might turn her around and she'd see, and she'd frown and say, "But didn't she have a face in back too? I thought . . ."

I grabbed Babe and laid her face up on the bed, draping the skirt and top over her pinkness. "See, this is going to be a wonderful fit."

"Lucky her. Probably a perfect size one half," Mom said, smiling, and I could tell she was glad to be finished with our talk about Dad. Talks about

Dad are always hard. I was glad, too. This terrible thought had come to me. Dad had left me. I'd left Babe. Not that the two things were the same, but . . .

"So bring Babe down with you when you get her dressed," Mom said. "There's a chicken casserole that I popped into the oven between clients, and it ought to be just about ready. You and Babe can set the table."

The doorbell rang.

"Who on earth?" Mom glanced at her watch. "I don't have any appointments tonight. Whoever it is, I'll be just a minute. Believe me, I've worked hard enough today. You go ahead and set the table and make the salad, will you?"

I heard her talking to someone at the door as I wiggled Babe II into the yellow skirt. How awful that had been. And I'd have to give Babe II a second face right away, because if Mom had noticed, what would I have said? Ellie might notice too, and what would Ellie say? She hated sneaky people. Ellie was so honest, she once found two pennies on the sidewalk outside school and took them into the office.

She would never believe I'd do something like this. I was her friend. Why was I doing it, anyway? I wasn't sure. But already I felt trapped, and suffocated. I stared down at Babe II's rosebud mouth and red-crayon curls.

"Vicki! Can you come here a minute?" That was Mom calling from downstairs.

I cradled Babe carefully in my arms. See what a good, conscientious, never-leave-her-alone mother I am?

Ophelia was in the hall with Mom. Ophelia? What was she doing here? All the guilt bubbled inside me again. Had Mr. Ambrose told her something after all? Babe II grew heavier and heavier, and my steps got slower and slower. "You *found* her," Ophelia would say. "I'm so glad. My dad was so worried." Or worse: What if she'd discovered the real Babe, upstairs in her house maybe. And she'd say, "What's that you've got? Have you *two* babies? I found one in . . ." I gripped the stair rail.

Ophelia and Mom were both looking up at me.

"Vicki?" Mom said. "Ophelia can't find her father. She wonders if you've seen him."

"I know you talked to him on the way home from school," Ophelia said. "I saw you as I was coming back from the market. Did he seem agitated to you?"

A-g-i-t-a-t-e-d. In a state of anxiety. We'd had it in spelling. It could also mean turning around and around, as in a washer. As in my stomach right now.

My throat was so dry I could hardly swallow, and I needed to swallow before I could speak.

"No," I whispered. "He wasn't agitated."

"He seemed really upset to me." Ophelia was squeezing her hands together in front of her, just the way her father had done when I said . . . when I said . . . Her face looked small and tight.

"Did you . . . did you check up on California Boulevard?" I asked, watching her hands pull at each other, watching and trying to make myself look somewhere else. Once before Mr. Ambrose had disappeared, and Ophelia had found him standing in the middle of a boulevard with traffic screeching around him while he waved and smiled.

She'd brought him home and tried to explain to him why it wasn't a good idea to go where there was traffic.

"He's not there. I've searched everywhere. I can't imagine . . ." Ophelia's face crumpled up.

Mom gathered her in a hug. "We'll find him, Ophelia. We will. Have you asked any of the other neighbors?"

Ophelia shook her head against Mom's shoulder. "I just came here. He and Vicki are such good friends."

I was clutching the sugar baby so tightly that

one of the seams I'd just sewn up split with a little plop. I set her down on the bottom step.

"Vicki," Mom said in a calm, reassuring way. "Get on the phone and call Mrs. Ting and Mrs. Coles and the rest of the neighbors. Someone may have seen him."

"He's got identification," Ophelia said as if talking to herself. "Everything's in his wallet. If anything happened, wouldn't someone call? My phone number's in there."

"Of course someone would call." Mom had her arm around Ophelia as she steered her toward a chair in the kitchen.

Ophelia pulled away. "I've got to go home. What if someone's trying to reach me right now?"

"I'll come with you," Mom said.

"Do you still want me to call people?" I asked. I'd never been so frightened in my life. Mr. Ambrose. Nice, sweet Mr. Ambrose. Had I done this? Had I been so rotten I'd made him run away? Should I tell? But I'd said I was sorry. Mr. Ambrose and I'd made up.

"Go ahead and make the calls, sweetie. It can't hurt," Mom said, and then Ophelia grabbed her arm. "Do you think I should call the police? They found him when he was lost that time before."

"Maybe that would be best," Mom said. "It might be safest."

The police? Worse and worse. I dropped the phone with a clatter against the wall. "Sorry," I muttered.

"I'll call them from Ophelia's," Mom whispered, and then she took Ophelia home while I began dialing all our neighbors—Mrs. Ting and Mrs. Coles, the minister on the corner and the dentist who lives in the house with the blue trim, and Mrs. Burch who writes poetry and does sculptings of horses and cowboys. Everyone knew Mr. Ambrose. No one had seen him.

All this because I'd wanted Thunk to like me. And in the end he hadn't even wanted our bikes to be chained together.

Mom had left the front door open and I was in the middle of one of the calls when I looked outside and saw a black-and-white police car cruising slowly past. They'd come.

11

All the neighbors had seen Mr. Ambrose earlier, in his usual spot, waving and smiling. They hadn't seen him since.

"You were talking to him when we passed this afternoon," Mrs. Coles said to me. "He didn't seem any different, did he?"

I curled and uncurled the telephone cord on my wrist. That's what Ophelia had asked. What kinds of questions were the police asking her? Would they come down here?

"He was just the way he always is, Mrs. Coles," I said. Then I added, because I couldn't help it, "The police are here. Mom called them."

"Oh." Mrs. Coles sounded doubtful. "She thinks that's necessary?"

"I guess."

Through the open door I saw a few of the neighborhood kids gathering on bicycles or skateboards. The kids for blocks around sense when a cop car comes, or the paramedics, or a fire truck. It's a kind of magic. "I'd better go," I told Mrs. Coles.

"Tell Ophelia to call me if there's anything I can do," she said. "I don't want to phone her in case I tie up her line."

"OK." I couldn't think of anyone else to call after that, so I hung up, got my pretend sugar baby, and went outside.

Ophelia and Mom and two policemen were standing in Mr. Ambrose's place. Seeing them there made him seem more missing than ever. Oh, Mr. Ambrose, where did you go? It wasn't because of me, was it? Say it wasn't.

Slowly I moved closer.

One of the policemen had something in his hand, and when I'd gone a few more steps I saw that it was a picture of Mr. Ambrose, taken when he was a bit younger, when he had more hair and his eyes were brighter behind his glasses. The smile in the picture was the same, though, and it made something catch in my throat.

"He was wearing gray pants and a blue knit shirt," Ophelia was saying in the strangest, tightest voice. I thought she sounded like the meringue on top of Mom's lemon pie, thin and crisp and ready to crack if you touched it. "I think he had on his dark-blue windbreaker, too," she said. "I could go check if it's gone from his closet." She looked past them then and directly at me. "Can you remember, Vicki? Did he have his windbreaker on when you saw him?"

I picked at the seam at the side of Babe II's head, the one that was unraveling. "I *think* he had it on," I said, and the policeman asked me when I'd seen him and I had to go over all that again, leaving out the bad parts, making today seem like every other day. Well, it had been like every other day. Except for the sweat on Mr. Ambrose's forehead and the way his words and his chin had quivered.

"Can you remember what the two of you talked about?" the policeman asked.

"Oh, nothing much. Just, you know, I said about school and he said about the weather." I looked down at my fake sugar baby. "And about this. My class project. Nothing important."

"Everything's important, no matter how small," the policeman said.

I shook my head and made myself look into his face. He had the scariest-looking mouth under his mustache, the kind that probably never smiled. I'd always thought it was silly to be afraid of policemen, but I was afraid now.

Mrs. Coles and Mrs. Ting came cruising up in Mrs. Ting's car, and Mrs. Coles said they thought they'd just drive around a bit and see if they could spot Mr. A. and was there any more news? That's what she called him—Mr. A.

There wasn't any news, of course.

But as soon as the policemen left, Mom said that she and I should go looking too, and we went back for our car. I could tell how worried Mom was because she didn't even lock our front door. She never leaves our house unlocked.

She and I drove all around. I remembered how frantically I'd searched for Babe earlier, but this was worse, much worse. We kept meeting Mrs. Ting's car and the Reverend Gish's. The Reverend and Mrs. Gish had joined the search too. We saw the cop car cruising slowly, soundlessly.

"Why don't they radio for a bunch more police?" I asked. "They need one of those Code Nines or whatever they call them."

"I imagine they'd wait awhile before they do anything like that," Mom said. "Maybe twenty-four hours."

"Twenty-four hours? That's terrible."

Mom gave a little shrug. "Probably most missing people come home on their own."

Oh, I hoped she was right.

We saw Thunk on his bicycle then, and I told Mom, "That's the boy from across the street," and Mom slowed up beside him. Thunk stopped with one foot on the curb. "I'm looking for the old guy, too," he said. "You don't need to go along this street 'cause I've checked it already and the next one down as well. Maybe you could go a couple of blocks the other way."

"Good idea," Mom said.

Thunk was still wearing the bicycle chain across his chest, the chain he'd used to lock us together and pull us apart. It didn't seem to matter that much anymore. I wondered if he and Cynthia had left the library at the same time, or if she'd stayed with her friend Harry Hogan. And that didn't matter either.

"Is your heart going pit-a-pat?" Mom asked as Thunk pedaled off.

"Not really," I said. Actually, it was. But this time it wasn't for Thunk. Not that he wasn't as cute as ever. But I had more important problems. Over and over inside my head I chanted, "Please, Mr. Ambrose. Please." Maybe I was begging him to show up. Or maybe to forgive me.

It seemed now as if the whole neighborhood had joined in the search. Just about all our save-the-library people had turned out. We'd lower our windows and call to each other, and Mom would keep widening our routes. One time Mrs. Gish called from her car, "I just can't imagine Mr. Ambrose not being at his post in the morning. I was saying to the Reverend how much we all take that fine old man for granted. He's like our sunshine here in California—lovely but not appreciated enough."

"That's the way we humans are," the Reverend Gish said in a solemn way. "A person is not missed until he's gone." I imagined that's the way the Reverend would sound when he was preaching a sermon, as if the end of the world was coming. It felt as if it was. The mournful way he'd said "gone" made me shiver.

It was almost dark now, and the street lights came on, filling the world with their pale-yellow glow.

"We're not going to find him," Mom said. "Wherever he is, he's far from home. It's twenty minutes to eight. I guess we'd better give up, Vicki."

We didn't talk as we drove back, and when we got to our house, we sat in the car, just sat and sat. It was as if going inside and shutting the door would shut Mr. Ambrose out forever.

"I don't know," Mom said wearily. "Poor Ophelia. And poor you." She put her hand over mine. "I know how much you love Mr. Ambrose."

"Do you remember when I was really little and I made him a chain of paper clips?" I asked. "It was before he got sick, remember? And he wore it to work the next day, hanging it around his neck on top of his tie. He looked so silly, and I told him it was OK to take it off and just wear it when he got home, but he wouldn't."

"I remember."

"And then it broke, and he lost all the clips. Remember how upset he was? I told him I'd make him a new one, but I never did." My stomach was beginning to hurt real bad. "What will happen now? I mean, it's night . . . and he's somewhere . . . and where will he sleep? He's all alone and . . ."

"There, honey—it's going to be all right," Mom said, pulling me close, cuddling me against her.

Around us the neighborhood dogs howled, sensing the activity, exciting each other in a frenzy of yaps and yelps. I wanted to yelp with them.

"Do you know what we need?" Mom asked. "We need to go in and eat something. Oh, drat—did I forget to turn off the oven? The casserole will be burned black."

But she had turned it off, and the casserole was cold again, so we opened a can of tuna and ate it with toast, and then Mom ran back up to Ophelia's to see if there was anything new.

When the phone rang, I thought it was Mom calling and that she had something good to report.

Mr. Ambrose was found. He was safe and tomorrow he'd be back, smiling and waving and giving out his daily weather bulletin.

I skidded across the kitchen floor to grab the receiver.

"Hello. Hello?"

There was silence and then a voice, low and scary, said, "It is night and I am coming."

"What?" I held the phone away, staring at it and then said, "Who is this?" My heart hammered with fright.

"The Count has arisen from his coffin. He needs his blo-ood," the dark, creepy voice said.

"The *Count*? Harry Hogan! Is that you?"

"Harry Hogan, is that you?" he repeated. "No, it isn't me. It isn't I, either. It's Dracula, and he's coming for that young Babe."

"Babe?" I didn't have Babe. I had a fake Babe in her place, and I'd lied and cheated and blamed Mr. Ambrose and now the whole world had toppled.

The tears that I'd kept inside all day wouldn't stay there anymore, and suddenly I was bawling and howling as loud as the dogs in the night.

On the other end of the line I heard Harry Hogan's faraway voice.

"Vicki? Vicki? What's the matter? I was only kidding. Drac's not coming for Babe. Honest. I'm not even allowed to go out this late. And he's not hungry anyway. He had hamburger for dinner. Vicki?"

He was still talking and I was still howling as I hung up the phone.

What if telling *would* somehow help find Mr. Ambrose?

That policeman had said even the smallest thing was important. And I had a feeling this wasn't small. But if I told, everyone would know about me, about the way I really was. I couldn't stand it. I fumbled my sunglasses out of my pocket and put them on. Oh, no What should I do?

12

Ophelia's door was propped open as if she hoped her father would walk in any second and she didn't want him to even have to turn the handle.

Mom and Ophelia sat together on the couch, as close to the phone on its little table as they could get. The room was still filled with the drifting scent of roses.

I guess I must have looked as weird as I felt, because Mom stood up when I blundered in and Ophelia did, too, but more slowly, holding onto the couch, her face as pale as paper. "What is it, Vicki? Did you find out something?"

"No." I rocked my make-believe sugar baby against me, swaying from side to side.

"What's wrong?" Mom came closer and bent to look into my face. "Why on earth are you wearing those sunglasses? It's nighttime."

I pulled the glasses off and stuffed them back into my pocket.

"Vicki, sweetheart, have you been crying again?" Her voice had that soft, caring feel to it, and I couldn't stand it.

"Don't be nice to me," I whispered. "It's all my fault. Oh, Ophelia, I'm so sorry. I did it. *I* made Mr. Ambrose go away."

Ophelia didn't seem to even hear me, but Mom did, and she said, a little impatiently, "Oh, stop it, Vicki. Ophelia doesn't need this kind of nonsense right now."

Every bit of me was shaking. I felt for my ears with my free hand, stuffing them under my hat. "I asked Mr. Ambrose to look after my baby . . . and maybe he lost her . . . or I think someone took her . . . I told him it was his fault and . . ."

"Your *baby?*" Ophelia was looking at me now as if I'd gone crazy.

"My sugar baby." I jiggled Babe II. "Not this one. The real one."

"Vicki," Mom said. "Calm down. You're not making sense. Start from the beginning and tell us what you think happened."

So I did. And I made myself not leave anything out just so I'd look better. "Then I went up to Mr. Gertmenian's market and bought another bag of sugar," I finished, staring down past Babe II at my dirty white tennies, their laces untied as usual, the daisy sticker that had looked so cool last week peeling off the side.

Mom felt behind her for a chair as if she'd gone suddenly blind or was so sick she couldn't see anymore. "Oh, Vicki," she said. "Vicki!" I'd never heard her say my name like that in my whole life.

"And I don't know what happened to my sugar baby either," I whispered. "Maybe someone's turned her into sugar cookies by now. Maybe they've eaten her. Maybe she's fudge." I turned up the fringe on Ophelia's rug with my toe, then turned it down again. There was such a terrible silence in the room and outside, too. Even the dogs had gone quiet, listening.

And then Ophelia spoke, her voice so loud and excited that it almost bumped me out of my skin.

"What did you say to him about the baby, Vicki? Tell me exactly."

"I . . . I said . . ." I swallowed, hating to have to go over again how rotten I'd been. "I told him it was his fault. That I'd left him in charge of my baby and—"

Ophelia held her arms wide and gave a little stork-like jump. "That's it. He's gone looking for the baby."

Mom had bounced up too, though I could tell she had no idea what Ophelia was talking about.

"I know where he is," Ophelia said. "I'm going right now to get him."

"You know?" Mom said. "Wait, Ophelia. Wherever it is, Vicki and I will come with you."

Ophelia was heading for the open door. "Have you got your purse?" Mom asked her. "Do we go in the car? Have you got your driver's license, Ophelia?"

"Oh. Oops." Ophelia ran to the table and grabbed her shoulder bag. Even so, when we got outside, Mom said, "Let me drive, Ophelia. Just tell me where we're going." Anyone with half an eye could see that Ophelia was in a nondriving state, but she was also in a nonlistening state, and she jumped right behind the wheel and turned the keys that she'd left in the ignition. Mom and I hardly had time to clamber in too, before we were in reverse, jerking out of the driveway and jouncing up the street.

I fastened my seat belt, staying quiet, hoping they'd forget I was in the back, hoping no one would remember to get mad at me, at least not for a while. I couldn't believe how calm I felt, though, as if something bad had risen out of me the way steam rises from a kettle. Whatever happened next couldn't be worse than what had happened already.

"Can you please tell us where we're going?" Mom

asked in the totally reasonable voice she uses when there's nothing reasonable going on.

"To Bleshnell's," Ophelia said.

Bleshnell's is one of our biggest and oldest department stores. We were going shopping?

We made such a tight turn at the corner that I felt the car wheels squeak against the curb. Both Mom's hands gripped the dashboard.

"Why to Bleshnell's?" she asked. I leaned forward to hear.

"Because once, when I was a baby . . . a toddler . . . my dad lost me in Bleshnell's. I can't remember, of course. But I heard about it plenty. . . . About how Dad was buying a lawn mower and how the salesman was showing him the way to hook up the grass catcher, and when Dad looked up, I was gone." We were stopped at a "left turn on green arrow only," and I sensed the car aching to leap forward under Ophelia's hands. Across the street, in the open mall, big against the dark of the mountains, was the lighted bulk of Bleshnell's.

"Come on, come on, arrow," Ophelia urged.

"You think your father remembers back that far?" Mom asked.

"He doesn't remember what happened yesterday

or last week," Ophelia said. "But his memories of a lifetime ago are absolutely clear. I'm betting your words brought it all back, Vicki."

I hugged the sugar baby tight. How far had he walked to get here? Did he have to ask the way or did he remember since it was a lifetime ago? How awful he must have felt.

"I'm so sorry, Ophelia," I whispered.

"I know you wouldn't hurt him on purpose, Vicki."

"But even so," Mom said, half turning, and I knew there'd be no escape from her later. But neither of us had worry left for anything but Mr. Ambrose now.

"What time is it?" Ophelia asked and answered herself, squinting down at the clock on the dash. "Ten minutes till nine. Ten minutes till closing. Come on, green arrow! Where are you?"

She glanced briefly through the rearview mirror at me. "Thank goodness you told us tonight, Vicki," and before I had a chance to say I should have told before, the arrow came on and we turned in front of the stopped traffic into the mall.

Bleshnell's parking lot was still half filled with cars, but Ophelia found a place close to the doors and the three of us rushed inside, bumping against people on their way out, most of them carrying the bright-yellow Bleshnell bag. Golden treasure bags, the ads called them.

Over the loudspeaker, a woman's voice caroled, "Ladies and gentlemen, five minutes till closing time. Thank you for shopping Bleshnell's."

"We'll split up," Ophelia said breathlessly. "Vicki, you take the escalator to the second floor. I'll go this way, you go that," she told Mom. "The lawn mowers used to be over here, to the left. I'm betting that's where Dad headed."

I could see across the whole floor as I rode up on the escalator. I could see Mom dashing through Men's Wear and Ophelia in Linens. I didn't see Mr. Ambrose. What if she was wrong? What if Mr. Ambrose hadn't remembered, hadn't come here at all? Babe II was suddenly so heavy that I let her rest on the moving handrail beside me, trying to smile back at the nice people coming down who admired her.

"How darling," a woman said, pointing Babe II' out to her little girl.

Why had I brought Babe, anyway? Why hadn't I left her in the car? Because I was on my honor to take her with me everywhere. Except that it was too late for my word of honor. And this was the wrong Babe. Please be here, Mr. Ambrose. Please.

The upstairs was almost empty. A salesclerk was folding a tumble of sweaters on a counter. Behind another counter, a lady tidied purses on a shelf.

"Can I help you?" she asked, glancing at her watch.

"No. It's OK. Except . . . have you seen an old gentleman around here anywhere?"

"I don't think so. Did you lose one?"

"Not exactly. He was probably waving, like this." I demonstrated and then said, "Never mind," and ran toward the next aisle. Two men, one of them carrying a golden Bleshnell's gift box, stepped out of my way. "Sorry," I gasped.

A salesclerk rang up change with a click and a clatter. A young guy rearranged dolls and stuffed toy animals in a big, open cupboard. And there was Mr. Ambrose, standing and watching, just the way he stands on our sidewalk. But he wasn't waving now. He wasn't smiling.

In the instant before I ran up to him, I thought, He lost Ophelia in the lawn mower department, but this was probably where he found her.

"Oh, Mr. Ambrose," I whispered.

"Looks like the sun's gone for the day," he said uncertainly, fumbling with the zipper on his blue windbreaker. And then he saw Babe II and smiled his sweet gap-toothed smile.

He thought I'd found my baby.

"Ophelia's here, Mr. Ambrose," I told him. "We can go home now." And I reached for his hand and held it against my cheek.

This time Ophelia let Mom drive while she sat in back with her dad, so the ride wasn't as hairy. But now that the big, awful worry of losing Mr. Ambrose was over, I had time again to worry about Babe, and about myself.

"Thank you so much, Vicki," Ophelia said as we got out of her car, and she smiled happily, as if I'd done nothing but wonderful things and was some sort of heroine. Ophelia is really nice.

"Don't be too hard on her, Beth," she said to Mom. "I imagine we did a few iffy things ourselves when we were her age."

But probably not this iffy, I thought.

"I hope you find your sugar baby, Vicki," she added.

I hoped so too, but I doubted it.

Mr. Ambrose waved us good-bye. "Wouldn't be surprised if it storms," he said, peering up at the cloudless, star-strewn sky.

Right now, I'd be surprised if it didn't.

13

Mom and I sat at our round kitchen table. Most of our important discussions have taken place at this table. I think King Arthur and his knights had the right idea. The table's a good place for important discussions because there are things to mess with so you don't have to look at the person opposite. There's the napkin holder, and the salt and pepper shakers, and the candle in its blue china candlestick.

"You know what you did was dishonest and wrong, Vicki," Mom said. "I'm not going to lecture you about it because I think the lesson was well learned. And I think what happened tonight was punishment enough."

I nodded, not looking up from fanning the napkins in their holder.

"Did you search for Babe? Really, really search?" she asked.

I nodded again.

"The two little kids, the Garcia boy and—?"

"I asked them. They didn't take her. And I checked everywhere on our street. I even went into Ophelia's and—"

"Did you check this house?"

"Babe's not here, Mom. Where could she be? Anyway, I left her with Mr. Ambrose right out there where anybody could steal her." I swallowed.

"Vicki, I know part of the reason you tried to cheat was because you want so much to see Keiko. That's right, isn't it?"

"Yes. But I didn't want an F. I'd hate to get an F. And I didn't want to look stupid in front of Mrs. Oda and the class, either. I'm sort of Mrs. Oda's pet, or one of them. I like her to like me."

Mom almost smiled. "I see we're going to have total honesty here."

I shrugged and poured a little stream of salt from the shaker into my hand. Thank goodness she didn't add "at last" to that honesty bit. That would have been awful.

"And what are you going to do about *her*?" Mom poked Babe II with her finger.

I'd left the sugar baby on the table between us. I wished I hadn't. She was a horrible reminder. Why hadn't I hidden her under my chair?

"I'm not going to turn her into cookies or fudge," I said. "She's not to blame for any of this. I'm going to keep her as a real sugar baby, forever and ever. Unless she turns moldy. But I'm not going to pretend she's the real Babe. I'll just tell everyone at school what I . . . you know . . . what I did." Carefully I divided the salt into two smaller piles. "How I . . . lost her."

"It's going to be hard, isn't it?" Mom said gently.

I bit my lip. "You don't think I have to tell how I made Mr. Ambrose get lost, too, and about how I . . . about how I planned to cheat?" I pulled the candle toward me and carefully picked off a wax drip.

"Oh, honey!" Mom leaned forward and took my hand in hers. "I don't believe you have to go that far. You told Ophelia and me. That was difficult enough, I know." She paused. "What's important is that you tell enough so you can feel true to yourself again. Do you understand, honey?"

I nodded.

Mom squeezed my hands. "Maybe I'm fooling myself, Vicki, but I don't think you would have gone through with the cheating part. Not when it really came to doing it."

I wasn't certain. I hoped she was right.

"About Keiko," she went on. "It seems—"

I interrupted. "I know I've proved I can't be trusted. You don't have to tell me."

"Vicki, you're eleven years old. You're not all grown up. That's what this proves. You looked for the easy way out instead of the right way. No, I won't let you go to take care of Keiko. But even if this hadn't happened, I don't think I would have allowed you to go."

I jiggled the pepper shaker and felt my nose tickle a warning.

"Do you hate me, Mom?"

"Hate you? Of course not, silly. I love you. And I'm proud of you for coming through in the end." She opened her arms. "Come here."

I came and sat on her lap, which isn't easy anymore since I'm such a lunk with my legs trailing on the floor and my arms as long as a gorilla's. But sitting on Mom's lap still feels good.

"So, it's bedtime," she said at last, pulling off my hat and smoothing my hair. "You can have the shower first. Be sure to leave me some hot water. I'll be up later to tuck you in."

"All right. Thanks, Mom. I love you, too."

Before I got in bed, I stood by my window, looking across the street at Thunk's house. Lights glowed in almost every window. The one above the porch that I thought might be his was dark, though, and wide open, the inside as mysterious as a cave. I'd never been in a boy's room except for my cousin

128

Salvo's, and his didn't count. His had smelled. Thunk's wouldn't.

Was he lying there asleep, his blue eyes closed, dreaming of Cynthia Sanders? He wasn't dreaming of me, that was for sure. I felt sad, in a numb sort of way. When I stood high on my tiptoes, I could see the roof of the Ambrose house. Inside, Mr. Ambrose was safe with Ophelia. But I still felt sad, and I began thinking more of those gruesome thoughts of Babe. The sprinklers in Thunk's yard suddenly came on, raining silver in the street lights. Oh, wherever Babe was, I hoped she wasn't lying abandoned on someone's grass, getting wet and turning into slurp.

For a minute more I stood, counting stars, picking out the face of the man in the moon the way I did for Keiko. "See, Keiko? Those are his eyes and there is his mouth." Thinking about Keiko made me sadder than ever. And I definitely could not think about tomorrow.

I was still standing there when Mom came upstairs.

"I haven't locked up yet," she said, standing close beside me. "I wanted to tell you something, Vicki. Tomorrow I'm going to call your father and suggest they send Keiko here for those two weeks. They could put her on a plane and we could meet her."

"Mom, oh, Mom! That would be so great. Keiko here? That would be even better."

"I doubt if you'd still get the hundred dollars from your father," Mom said, her voice teasing.

"I might," I said quickly. "I'd still be baby-sitting days. You'd let me, wouldn't you, if you were here?"

Mom smiled. "Happy to."

Reflected in the window I could see the two of us, shimmery soft, somehow beautiful.

"Will you mind a whole lot, Mom? I mean, I know it's hard for you with Keiko . . . hard to deal with Dad."

"Maybe it will get easier if I put more effort into it." Mom gave my shoulder a little nudge the way Ellie does sometimes. "Anyway, it's not your *dad* I'm inviting. I'm not ready for that yet, kiddo."

We smiled at each other in our window mirror. "That's OK," I said.

It wasn't until I was in bed, listening to Mom finally locking the downstairs doors, rattling the chain in the lock, that I remembered another awful thing. Tonight Horrible Harry Hogan had called me, for some weird reason, and I'd cried on the phone. He'd heard me, too. There was no way he could have missed that. How humiliating.

I burrowed into my pillow, then came out again

because someone was calling, "Vicki! Vicki!" It was Mom, downstairs, her voice so excited and urgent that I threw off the bedcovers and jumped with my heart hammering. "What, Mom? What happened?"

"Come fast, Vicki! You'll never believe what I found."

Even as I raced down the stairs, I knew. But how could it be? "Where are you, Mom?"

"Here. In the dining room."

I ran in.

Our side patio opens off the dining room. There's an outside light, and Mom had switched it on while she checked the locks, the way she does every night. She stood sideways to me now, glancing back at me, then pointing outside.

I raced over beside her. There was the dusty glass patio table, the four white metal chairs, the plants in their pots. And, carefully hidden from the driveway, between the big rubber tree and the wall, was Babe. Snug in her basket, she smiled happily up at us.

"Oh, Babe!" I squeezed past Mom, lifting my sugar baby, cuddling her against me. "Oh, I'm so glad to find you. Are you all right? But how did you get here? How did she get here?" I asked Mom.

"I bet Mr. Ambrose brought her as soon as you

left today. He was taking good care of your baby, hon, just the way you asked him to, tucking her safely out of sight. But then he didn't remember."

"Oh, criminy!" I collapsed into one of the chairs.

"Don't sit there," Mom said automatically. "You'll get your pj's dirty." Then she came out and sat in one of the chairs herself, beaming across at Babe and me. "I'm really glad for you, Vicki. Really, really glad."

"I guess tomorrow's not going to be so bad after all," I said. "But I still have to tell what happened, don't I? I mean . . ."

I let the sentence trail away, hoping Mom would finish it for me, hoping maybe she'd say, "I don't see why. Nobody knows your sugar baby was even missing. Why tell them?"

But of course she wasn't going to say that. Whatever I did tomorrow was going to be entirely up to me.

14

I got up very early the next morning because I had things to do.

Babe and I were ready when Ellie came. I noticed right away that she was wearing her sister Cam's silver belt, the one like Cynthia Sanders'.

"I see your sugar baby has a nice, new outfit," Ellie said. "She looks terrific."

I picked a piece of lint off Babe's pink corduroy skirt and top. "Thanks." I hadn't changed Babe II's clothes this morning, but I'd promised her I would when I got back from school. And I'd told Teddy to keep her company till I got home.

"I'm sorry now I made Sweet Sam be Superman," Ellie said. "I bet he's bored to death with his crazy outfit. I know I am."

We were passing Mom's office window and we called good-bye.

"Like my new purple socks?" Ellie asked, lifting a foot. "I got them yesterday." Before I could answer, she spotted the extra thing in Babe's basket and bent to inspect it. "What's this?"

"A paper-clip chain," I said. "It's for Mr. Ambrose."

"How come?"

"Because." I took out the chain and let it hang from my fingers.

Mr. Ambrose was at his post, waving to Stumpy the cat, who was setting off on the day's prowl. As soon as he saw us, Mr. A. changed his waving direction.

"Lovely morning," he called.

"Yes," I said. And it was, with the sun wavering through a golden haze and a million birds flickering in the magnolia trees.

Now he had noticed the chain and his smile got wider.

"This is for you," I told him, and he bent toward me while I slipped it over his head and fixed it to hang straight.

He nodded and smiled even more.

"See you after school," I told him. "I have lots of important stuff to tell you. 'Bye."

Ellie and I walked backward so we could keep waving all the way to the corner.

"What's the important stuff?" Ellie asked. "And

where were you last night? I called your house four times. First the line was busy and then there was no answer. I got in a lot of trouble for hogging the phone, and Carol and I had a big fight."

Carol is Ellie's sister who is fifteen and who makes a career out of talking on the phone to her boyfriend, Chase. Chasing Chase, Ellie and I call it. "Did you and your mom go someplace?" Ellie asked.

I glanced at her sideways, feeling the tightness come again in my stomach. Mom hadn't hated me when I'd told her what I'd done. But a mom can't very well give up on her daughter. A friend probably could.

"It's a long story," I said. "It started when Thunk asked me to go to the library with him and—"

"Oh, wow!" Ellie was totally boggled. "You went, of course. Was he super adorable? What did you talk about?"

"Wait, wait!" I told her about Cynthia being there with Horrible Harry Hogan. "She's not really as bad as we thought she was," I said. "She probably can't help being a magnet. And I could tell she likes Harry Hogan." This part of the telling was easy, and I was in no hurry to rush through it.

Ellie stared at me, wide-eyed. "You mean *likes*? As in *s-e-r-i-o-u-s*?"

"Of course not. She's in seventh grade and he's only in sixth. She couldn't be s-e-r-i-o-u-s."

Ellie took a deep breath. "I don't see why not. If it's OK for a girl, for *girls*, in sixth grade to like a boy in seventh, I guess it would work the other way around, too."

"I bet she thinks he's just a kid," I said. "No seventh grader would ever *seriously* notice a sixth grader."

We walked a few steps without speaking and then I asked, "Did you hear what I just said?"

"I heard," Ellie said sadly. "And it's probably true."

I nodded. "I think I figured that out at the library yesterday."

"You know what?" Ellie asked after another long, meaningful silence. "If Harry Hogan was a seventh grader, I bet Cynthia would really like him. Harry Hogan is terribly cute."

I stopped to face her. "*Our* Harry Hogan? Are you kidding?"

"He has very nice arms," Ellie said. "Didn't you ever notice?"

"Definitely not. Did I tell you he called me last night?"

"Again? No kidding, Vicki? Maybe he really likes you."

I felt my ears getting hot. I think they do that because they get so little protection from my hair. "He doesn't *like* me," I said. "Just stop it, Ellie."

"OK, OK." Ellie rolled her eyes. "So after you—" She stopped. "Oh, criminy! He's coming. Thunk!" Quickly she transferred Sweet Sam's basket from her left hand to her right so it would be less noticeable. "There's no place to hide our babies."

"It doesn't matter. After all, we're only sixth graders. No use trying to impress him."

Thunk stopped beside us. "I see the old guy got back. Mom said you found him in a department store?"

"Yes."

He peered into Babe's basket. "Is this one of those baby projects?"

"We wouldn't do stupid stuff like this if we didn't have to," Ellie said, picking up the trailing end of her silver conch belt and swinging it nonchalantly.

I gave her a look. Thunk didn't seem to notice either her belt or my look.

"We had to carry eggs," he said. "I dropped mine the second day. Got an F." He grinned that adorable white grin. "See you!"

We watched him ride off.

Ellie sighed. "And to think he was once a sixth

grader. Anyway, we sure have good taste in older men."

"And next year we'll be older too," I said. "Here comes Tina Fisher."

Tina was groaning loudly as she caught up with us, pulling the red wagon that held her twins, C and H.

"These kids have me totally exhausted," she said. "I was up half the night with them. As soon as C starts crying, H joins in. It drives me crazy."

Usually I'm not that glad to see Tina Fisher, but I was now. With her here, Ellie wouldn't expect me to finish the story. I could put it off for a little longer.

Mrs. Oda smiled down at me from behind her desk. "Good morning, Vicki."

"Good morning, Mrs. Oda." I set Babe's basket carefully on the floor.

"Dracula is very hungry this morning," Harry Hogan whispered close against the back of my head. "He's dreaming of that sweet Babe blood, licking his lips, sharpening his teeth—"

"Stop it, Harry Hogan," I whispered, but not as forcefully as usual. I had too much on my mind. And it was such a relief that at least he wasn't advertising the way I'd cried on the phone. Maybe he hadn't heard after all.

"Are you teasing Vicki again, Harry Hogan?" Mrs. Oda asked.

"No, Mrs. Oda," Harry said. "It's Dracula. He wants to take a bite out of Babe."

"Oh, really?" Mrs. Oda perched herself on the edge of her desk. She was wearing a red blouse with a string of glass beads, and her red shoes had darling little bows at the toes. Ellie had already drawn my attention to them by coughing and pointing secretly under the desk. But today I wasn't even that interested in Mrs. Oda's shoe bows. I glanced around the room. Everybody had a sugar baby. I was going to be the only one with a confession. Did I have to confess everything? I was dreading it, dreading it.

"You know, Vicki," Mrs. Oda was saying, "I think Dracula must have a crush on Babe. Boys only tease girls they have crushes on. Didn't you know that?"

I shook my head, not caring.

"Harry Hogan teases Vicki Charlip all the time," Jimmy Silverado yelled.

"Shut up," Harry Hogan yelled back. But now everyone was pointing at him and laughing and saying, "Harry likes Vicki. Harry likes Vicki.

139

Harry Hogan's blushing. Harry Hogan's blushing."

Mrs. Oda held two fingers high in the air, which is what she does when we're rowdy and she needs to get our attention.

"I'm going to take attendance for once," she said. "We have to keep these records formal." When we all answered, she took sugar baby attendance. Then she asked, "Does anyone have anything to report about sugar baby care?"

A bunch of hands went up, but not mine. My heart had started to beat awfully fast.

Tina Fisher jabbered some more about her twins and explained that they were the reason she hadn't been able to finish her homework. She'd die if she knew I had twins too. Jeremiah Green said his new puppy had gotten ahold of his sugar baby, Miss Dolly. And then he showed the two Band Aids on Miss Dolly's stomach. "Emergency surgery," he said. "But she's going to pull through."

"She's thinner," Mrs. Oda said. "She's lost weight."

"She lost sugar," Jeremiah explained.

I waited till everyone had said what they had to say before I put up my hand. And I didn't put it up very high.

"Yes, Vicki?" Mrs. Oda asked.

I stood, the way the others had done. How could

my stomach feel so empty? It wasn't that long since breakfast. "I left Babe with . . . with someone who couldn't take care of her very well, and so . . . so she was missing for seven hours."

I thought I heard Harry Hogan whisper, "Take it easy," behind me, but maybe I only imagined it.

"See?" Barbara Sandberg said into the interested silence. "You should never leave your baby with someone irresponsible. You should have asked me. I'm a licensed care person. Did I give you my card?" She rustled around in her backpack.

"I'm sorry to hear about this, Vicki," Mrs. Oda said. "Is there more?"

I nodded.

"The man . . . he's my friend but he's sort of sick . . . he was so upset at losing Babe that he went looking for her and he got lost himself."

"Did you find him?"

"Yes. And my sugar baby, too."

Mrs. Oda held the end of her glass beads thoughtfully against her lips.

"I would have given you one of my twins," Tina Fisher said. "Two babies are too much work."

"Thank you for sharing this, Victoria," Mrs. Oda said. "There's a valuable lesson here for all of us."

"Will she get an F?" By the enthusiastic way

Jeremiah Green asked, I could tell he hoped I would. Jeremiah Green gets lots of Fs himself, and he'd be glad of some company.

"That's not your concern, Mr. Green," Mrs. Oda said. "Our sugar baby project was to help us learn responsibility. There are all kinds of responsibility. Admitting your mistakes is one." She smiled at me. "You may sit down now, Vicki."

It was so strange. My legs kept twitching, encouraging me to sit, but then they'd stiffen and keep me standing. Maybe they were getting different signals. Maybe they didn't know what to do because I didn't know myself. So far nobody had been too disgusted with me. But that was because they didn't know everything. I should stop now. Mom had said I didn't need to confess the whole story. Sit, I told my legs, sit! Keep quiet! I told my mouth. But the words came out anyway.

"I bought another bag of sugar. I fixed it up to look like Babe. I was going to bring her to school."

Mrs. Oda's face changed. I couldn't look at her anymore. I watched my fingers space themselves flat on the top of my desk. There was a lot of whispering.

"That was pretty smart," someone said from the back of the room. I thought it was Jeremiah Green.

Ellie had turned to look at me, her mouth an O of horror.

"You were going to cheat?" Mrs. Oda asked.

I nodded. "But then we found Babe. This is the real Babe, honest, Mrs. Oda. See where she has a face in back and—"

Ellie jumped up. "Vicki wouldn't have cheated even so, Mrs. Oda, even if she hadn't found Babe. I know she wouldn't."

I had my head bent, studying my fingers, but I flashed a quick look and a quick smile at Ellie, who was all pinked up now.

Thank you, Ellie. Thank you. Two people believed in me. Mom and Ellie. And they were two people who knew me pretty well.

"And what do *you* think, Victoria?" Mrs. Oda's voice was as soft as Mom's had been last night.

I shrugged, watching my fingers again.

"Well, I don't think you would have cheated either," Mrs. Oda said.

Three believed in me. Three.

"Anyone with the courage to stand in front of me and the whole class and say what you said when you didn't have to isn't a cheat at heart."

"Thank you," I whispered, and this time when I told my legs to let me sit, they did.

"Take out your notebooks, students," Mrs. Oda said in her absolutely everyday voice, as though nothing out of the ordinary had happened. I heard my heart slip back into its normal beat. Was it over? Was it all over?

"I thought we might write sugar baby birth notices to go in the school paper," she said. "I'll print a sample one on the board."

"Pretty soon we'll be writing *death* notices," Judy Petrone said. "My mom wants Corky back on Saturday. We're going to have homemade ice cream."

"Oh, yuk. Grosso."

George Cuesta began to ping out a tune on his retainer. It was the sad trumpeter call that's played at the graves of dead heroes.

I slumped a little in my seat. It *was* over. Oh, thank goodness. "Are you OK?" Ellie whispered, giving me a sympathetic smile. I nodded and opened my notebook. And the first thing I saw was the family tree I'd drawn yesterday. Keiko! I began to imagine her here, Mom and me taking her to Kidspace and to feed the ducks at the Arboretum.

"Vicki?" Harry Hogan tapped my shoulder.

"What?" When I turned, I saw that he was holding a folded paper.

"Hey! Harry Hogan's passing Vicki Charlip a love

144

note," Tina Fisher said. Honestly, Tina isn't so busy with her twins that she misses anything.

"It's *not* a love note," Harry Hogan said. "It's last year's program of *Beauty and the Beast.* Cynthia Sanders asked me to give it to Vicki."

I nodded forcefully, holding up the program with Cynthia's face smiling from the cover. "I'm going to use it for play publicity," I said.

"Some *fox*!" Jeremiah Green gave the kind of whistle Ellie and I *say* we think is disgusting. We have, however, admitted to one another that we hope someone whistles at us like that, at least once in our lifetimes.

A smaller piece of paper fluttered down from the middle of the program. I snatched it up before anyone could see.

"Count Dracula would like to take Miss Babe to the movies Friday night (not tomorrow night but the next)," I read. I guess the Count or Harry Hogan had put in "(not tomorrow night but the next)" in case I didn't know when Friday was. "Drac promises to keep his fangs out of Miss Babe's neck. P.S. The movie is *Tex*, and it's hot."

I sat looking at the words, snorting softly. Did Harry Hogan mean I was to bring Babe to the movies, and he'd bring Dracula and we'd all sit together?

Did that mean this was a date? Was this just his weird way of asking? A date! I began to get an excited, jumpy feeling inside. Two phone calls and a s-e-r-i-o-u-s date! Wait till I tell Ellie.

I checked my ears, then got my pen and wrote "Miss Babe accepts Count Dracula's invitation for Friday (not tomorrow night but the next)."

I held the note over my shoulder close to where my right ear would have been if I hadn't tucked it in. Maybe I could wear my hat Friday? But why bother? After sitting behind me since first grade, Harry Hogan had seen my ears lots of times.

I saw his hand come up to take the note, and I turned my head just a little bit more. And believe it or not, Ellie was right. Harry Hogan has very nice arms.

ABOUT THE AUTHOR

Eve Bunting is the winner of the 1976 Golden Kite Award and the recipient of the 1977 Best Work of Fiction Award of the Southern California Council on Literature for Children and Young People. She has written over one hundred books for children, including *Is Anybody There?*, which was nominated for an Edgar Award in 1989. She is also the author of five Lippincott Page-Turners, including *The Haunting of SafeKeep* and *If I Asked You, Would You Stay?*, a 1984 Best Book for Young Adults (ALA) and a 1985 High Interest/Low Reading Level Book (ALA).

Ms. Bunting was born in Ireland and since 1958 has lived with her husband and three children in Southern California, where she works as a teacher and lecturer.